The Farewell Tree

Mert Urkmez

The Farewell Tree

HISTRIA
FICTION

Histria Fiction

Las Vegas ◊ Chicago ◊ Palm Beach

Published in the United States of America by
Histria Books
7181 N. Hualapai Way, Ste. 130-86
Las Vegas, NV 89166 USA
HistriaBooks.com

Histria Fiction is an imprint of Histria Books. Titles published under the imprints of Histria Books are distributed worldwide.

Library of Congress Control Number: 2024931087

ISBN 978-1-59211-456-6 (softbound)
ISBN 978-1-59211-462-7 (eBook)

For my parents
Metin and Nebahat

Part 1

'Only the mind of a slave condemns suicide. Cherish our freedom!' read the ornate marble arch built last summer at the entrance of the city park to commemorate fifty years of peace since the Great War. Next to the arch stood a yellow placard with bold red letters reminding people to show up at the upcoming referendum three months later: 'Enshrine our right to suicide in the Constitution! Vote for the freedom.'

It was the first time Saul stepped into the park, and although a couple of minutes had barely passed, he already hated it. Nevertheless, now he was standing under the marble arch whose interior city artists had decorated with gruesome yet elegant depictions of people ending their lives in various manners, ranging from a girl jumping from a height to a man taking more pills than prescribed by his physician.

If it wasn't for his girlfriend Poppy's incessant requests to celebrate her eighteenth birthday here, he would never have stepped inside the park. Despite all his whining, pleading, and even threatening, he couldn't change her mind as she shot down each one of his proposals with a disarming smile. But above all, he had to concede defeat when he failed to tell her why he was so fiercely trying to avoid having a picnic with their classmates here.

Saul's entire body was tensing up, even though his soft facial features contrasted by a strong jawline stayed unfazed to mask his unease. His dark eyes were trying to cut through the forest to see what lay in front of him.

'Good thing for you the law wasn't passed last year,' Poppy said, lowering her sunglasses from her head and running her fingers through her wavy hair.

'Don't get it started again. Besides, maybe it won't pass this year either. You know we're campaigning for it,' Saul said, trying to assure himself more than her. 'People can change their minds. Have a little faith in democracy, Plato. Actually, you should come with me to the meeting tomorrow,' Saul said and turned around to face his girlfriend, but Poppy simply reacted with an exhale and a smirk. 'Stop making fun of it, Poppy! We can save people.'

'I told you it's a waste of time. Nothing would change if the no vote was six percent instead of five,' Poppy said and walked past Saul, still dragging him by the hand. 'Besides, no one needs your saving, Don Quixote. I have more important things to do.'

'Such as playing with your dollhouse?' Soon after Saul finished his question, Poppy hit his diaphragm with her open left palm.

'Such as going to my karate training?' The hit almost knocked the wind out of Saul, who hunched and fell into a coughing fit. 'Pray, I didn't close my fist,' Poppy said and fixed her dress.

'I… deserved… that,' Saul wheezed, still trying to catch his breath.

'You did. No more politics. Don't embarrass me today. You know I hate Luna,' Poppy said, grabbed Saul's chin, and gave him a little kiss. 'I love you.'

'No doubt,' Saul mumbled under his breath, still massaging his chest.

'I didn't catch that,' Poppy said and turned around one more time to face her boyfriend.

'I said I love you too.'

'Much better. Aren't you glad we came?' Poppy said, then threw her hands to the sides and drew a big breath. Then, in a quick, elegant move, she leaned forward to take off her shoes and started jumping in circles on the grass around him. Twirling with each step, her blue summer dress, which was adorned with summer flowers, met the wavy chestnut hair on her pale shoulders, creating a natural amalgamation of the lake and forest in her image.

Although Saul was still thinking, '*The weather is nice in other places also; I'd have been glad if we'd gone anywhere else*,' he preferred to keep the thoughts to himself, as any objection at this point would be futile apart from further infuriating Poppy on her birthday and creating the risk of more bodily harm for himself. So, he sufficed by throwing a forced grin her way and picked up her small shoes lying on the ground.

But he was afraid of this park. With every step he took inside, his lungs were shrinking, leaving him almost gasping for air; his soul was trapped in a man with a fear of heights being dragged to the edge of the cliff while the last drops of courage were fleeting away from him, giving way to the irresistible call of the void.

As if to mock him, the park was brimming with life. Families and friends, huddled around the banks next to the lake, were enjoying the last days of the spring, yielding their time to the summer. New parents were struggling to push their strollers on the uneven surface while searching for a shade to rest in. The toddlers played hide and seek, as elder siblings kept an eye on unleashed dogs that were frantically looking for their toys or simply chasing an unfortunate butterfly while running away from their owners. Across the commotion rising from the banks, where trees gave way for a small opening, a group of little kids were running beside a young boy who was trying to make his kite fly. After a few trials, a sudden gust of wind decided to lend a hand and lifted the kite momentarily above their heads.

'You have to loosen the string. Let it fly!' One of the kids' fathers shouted with a booming voice from the bench while clenching not his first beer in his paws. But before the kids could oblige with the instructions from the mustached man with the pork belly, the wind had subsided as quickly as it started, dashing the hopes of a quick success. Now, people lined around the lake and under the shade of the trees, put a pause on their lazy conversations, and diverted their attention to the kid with the bright red kite.

The owner of the kite picked up his toy once more to run with his friends to breathe new life into it. This time, to the delight of the mustached gentleman with the belly, the kid managed to let the string loose on time, and the kite started flying toward the sky. Beaming with excitement and full of pride in accomplishing the task, the kids began clapping to encourage the kite to sail even higher to compete with the birds circling the woods. Once the string reached its full length and the red kite turned into a dot above the woods, people in the park were already captivated by its magic, failing to break their gaze from the distant red blur for fear of being the one causing its inevitable demise. The red kite, in an open rebellion against the fate written for it, was comfortably sailing in the sky, devoid of the memories of its coy beginnings. It seemed that if the kids let go of the silver lifeline keeping the kite grounded, it wasn't going to fly away but simply land on a branch atop a tree to start chirping to woo a mate of its own before Spring ended.

When Saul freed himself from the magic of the kite, his gaze locked on the back of his girlfriend, who was still enjoying the kite's flight. He felt a sudden urge to hug her tightly from behind, bury his face in her slender neck, and let her warmth rid his heart of anxieties. Before he took a step, she swiftly turned around to lock her eyes with him, washing away all the worries, even if only momentarily.

'Let's walk around the lake to the north. I can see a free bank there,' Poppy said and, with an energetic gait, started walking to the bank while eyeing whether someone else was on their way to steal their spot. As the pair was rushing to the bank before anyone else, Poppy was rubbing the back of her hand to Saul's, encouraging him to lock fingers. Starting to shiver with the expectation of what was lying in front of him, Saul shirked his gentlemanly obligation, hid his hands in his pockets, and clenched his jaw to embrace for the impact. 'If I am to die today or tomorrow or even this week,' Saul whispered to himself, 'I would like to die rather earlier but quickly now.'

'I didn't catch it.'

'Nothing.'

'If you don't want to hold my hand,' Poppy said with childish indignation in her voice and took a step forward to turn and face Saul, 'I can easily find another willing boy,' with a twinkle in her eye, alleviating the gravity of her threat.

On another day, even the veiled implication of such a prospect would have caused his blood to evaporate out of his ears. But this was another special day in itself. With each step forward, he was expecting to face the void, but now, suddenly, the void became omnipresent. A gazelle circled by a pride of lions, he was transfixed to what was towering in front and inside him: The Farewell Tree.

***

No one had planted the Farewell Tree. This oak tree, a spider with hundreds of legs sprawling the sky from dawn to dusk, was here before the other trees, chestnuts, or saplings that were aspiring to see the sunrise. Its trunk, around which five kids could play hide and seek, was shooting boughs as thick as bear waists, adorned with emerald butterflies dancing with the breeze to the backdrop of the azure sky. The Farewell Tree's roots were sprawling as an invisible testament to old days gone by that no one saw with their own eyes in the city, yet felt a yearning for.

Then, over one of its nondescript branches hung a steel noose. Forged a long time past, the steel noose was sliding on itself without any lubrication because of its smooth stem. Connecting to the stem in a circle was a saw which aimed, unlike its rope cousin, not to crush the neck but to sever the head. Below the noose stood a five-step earthen stairwell that led to nowhere. Regularly maintained and inspected by the city, the noose and the staircase were preserved in pristine condition. At each appointment, cleaners meticulously scrubbed, dried and polished the noose to prevent the onset of rust.

That day, one municipality worker was mowing the grass around the tree while another was inspecting the sharpness of the noose using a magnifying glass and making minor corrections with sandpaper to make sure everything was according to the standards.

'Let's wrap it up. The next appointment is almost here.' the inspector said and asked his colleague to hurry. 'You know no one likes to wait.'

***

Theo didn't enjoy being a driver for the passenger rail, as he found the job increasingly annoying because of the regular jumpers in front of the trains. 'Ah. Great!' he used to say every time he saw someone standing on the tracks. He would slap his bald head and tug on his long, red bushy beard. 'There goes my lunch.' He would then punch the side window of the cabin and slam his fist on the dashboard right before the impact, 'Selfish bastard.'

'C'mon, girl. Try driving yourself now,' Theo said and pointed to the intern to take his seat. 'You won't learn by staring.'

'I am not sure I'm ready. Shouldn't we wait until we stop at a platform at least?' the girl replied, took a step back from Theo, and pressed herself against the cabin door.

'You completed the theory classes already. Now it's time,' Theo said and stood up from the chair. The reluctant girl squeezed past between Theo's belly and the dashboard to take control of the train. She drew in a big breath and grabbed the stick with her trembling hands.

'Don't need to squeeze it. It won't be running away,' Theo said and shook his head. He then rechecked the schedule. 'Hmm. If we go fast enough, I might be able to switch to the O-Train after lunch.'

Jumpers had become so much of a public nuisance that the municipality had to invest in a new train line that was only for people to kill themselves without delaying fellow commuters who were growing more and more agitated by the occasional announcement coming over the speakers in the platforms: 'May I have your attention, please. We are sorry to announce that the next train will be delayed because of a jumper. We apologize for the inconvenience this may cause you.' The announcement always caused a stir among the passengers waiting on the platform.

'I can't believe how selfish people are! I am going to be late for my meeting. Second time this week!'

'Hey! It's well in their right. Blame the municipality for being incompetent. They were delaying the jumper train for almost a year now!'

Theo had immediately asked his supervisor to switch to the new train line as a driver. *No more delays,* he thought. Days were much calmer in his new job. There were even days he conducted the train on empty tracks with no jumpers. But those were increasingly rare. Although some people had initially insisted on jumping in front of the passenger trains, through extensive campaigning efforts, more and more jumpers decided to be responsible citizens and switched over to the new line that was exclusively for them.

Usually, the people waited for him on the tracks. Half of them were directly facing him. Theo didn't like those. Especially the chummy ones who waved. He preferred people who turned their backs to the incoming train. But the worst were the ones who waited on the platform and idled, trying to muster their courage. For those jumpers, the municipality had recently hired 'motivators' whose task was to push the people who asked for help as they could not find the courage themselves. Before the motivators, Theo would be nervous each time he passed by the mock platform and wondered whether the person would jump. He appreciated the pushers. 'It is a tough job,' he said to his wife. 'If they push too early, people would slam their face on the ground and needlessly hurt themselves before I come. But if they push too late, the person might just slam on the side and survive, most likely with a disability.' He shook his head. 'Then they have to kill themselves for sure. As soon as possible. No one can live like that.'

As he needed to drop off his daughter for an appointment that day, he had to ask his supervisor for a change in his schedule. Unfortunately for him, Theo's supervisor assigned him to a passenger train and asked him to take an intern on the train for training.

'Take the girl along with you,' the supervisor said, pointing to the pony-tailed girl sitting outside his office. 'She completed the theory and now should start driving.'

'Do we let the girls be drivers now also?'

'Why not?'

'You're right. Why not?'

Every time they arrived at a platform, he was uneasy. Every time the train approached a station, he squinted and tried to scan the crowd for a potential jumper. He pulled out the schedule and checked the route for the next station.

'We're going to skip the incoming station, and the one after that is the last stop. Time for lunch,' Theo said and checked his watch again. 'Maybe I can still make it to the O-train.'

'Will I get to drive the O-train also?'

'With this speed, you would barely maim people. We shouldn't drop below seventy on average. If we're late, I'll ask for you to be failed. C'mon girl!' The intern grunted but pushed the stick, and the train picked up speed. Invisible to her, Theo nodded with approval, as her confidence impressed him. Something his daughter had not had. 'Why did you choose to be a driver, anyway?'

'To have friendly colleagues.'

'Ha! Ha! Good one. Eyes on the track. Check the dashboard.'

'How about you?' the intern asked and lowered her shoulder. For the first time now, she rested her back on the chair and pushed the stick up higher. The wheels vibrated a bit more, and the train picked up speed.

'Unionized job with a good pay. What else there is to ask for in life?'

'Maybe a bit more than that, but sure, those sound good,' she replied and straightened her back again. 'Should I lower the speed? We're approaching a station.'

'No. Let's keep going. Nobody will complain if we arrive a bit early.'

As the train approached the platform, Theo again tried to scan the crowd, whose faces disappeared under a blur, revealing no intention whatsoever on their part. Just as the train reached the end of the platform and he breathed a sigh of relief, a man pushed another in front of the oncoming train.

Blood sputtered up in the air and covered the cabin's windshield. Theo reached over the screaming intern and pulled the brake, but the train dragged on for another thirty seconds. 'Well. That's a first,' Theo said. He then slapped his bald head, then tugged on his red beard, and let out a loud groan. 'Amazing! There goes our lunch. Here comes an extra thirty minutes of scrubbing. Damn it! Stop screaming, girl!'

***

Now, their friends, along with a basket of sandwiches and cakes they brought, had joined them around the bank for Poppy's birthday celebration. Grant, an athletic forward and a teammate of Saul from the football team, lit a cigarette, enjoying a freedom he earned mere months ago.

'We have a nice angle, and it seems we've missed nothing yet,' Grant pointed with his head towards the Farewell Tree. Laughing at his own remark, he combed his light blond hair back and blew out the smoke. Either displeased with her boyfriend's observation or smoke hitting her face, Luna rolled her eyes and puffed, 'We were late because we forgot the candles for the cake. Luckily, when we picked up Ezra, he told us he had an extra package at home,' Luna said, playing with the tips of her long blonde hair. '*How strange!*' Saul thought to himself. '*They look more like siblings than lovers.*'

Ezra pulled the candles from his pocket and passed them on to Grant's sister, sitting next to Poppy. Saul noticed that among their friends, Ezra, who was sitting silently, twiddling his thumbs, was the only one who seemed uneasy being there. He wondered whether he was just projecting how he felt onto his old friend. But it was clearly apparent that the presence of the tree bothered no one else at the table or even in the entire park. They accepted it as a natural fact of life. But not Ezra. But not Saul.

Saul and Ezra had known each other since kindergarten. They had always been best friends, teammates, and partners in crime. But since they had started high school and Saul had Poppy in his life, an invisible wedge began to push them apart. He could not remember when they had just drunk something on a laid-back afternoon to discuss their dreams, laugh at jokes they came up with years ago, and plan where they wanted to travel in the world once they had the time and money.

Saul thought to himself that this was the worst way to lose a friend. 'You do not fight, argue, or even go your separate ways, but just lose interest in each other and stop talking. Maybe this was a natural process of growing up. As snakes grow, they shed their old skin that is restricting them to give way to new colorful scales. Like snakes, maybe people needed to shed old dreams, friends, and ambitions to make way for new ones. But my friend is not just a piece of skin to get rid of by slithering over a rock. Why would growing up require one to give up their friends and dreams? Life should instead be like a bird building its nest by surrounding itself with the most beautiful and sturdiest branches it meticulously picks up each and every day. Then a man should be able to surround himself with new friends, new dreams by building upon the ones he already has.' Saul felt ashamed of himself for even thinking about removing his friend from his life. He promised himself to take Ezra out and spend an evening with him.

'I can't comprehend how people put up with the hassle of coming here to commit suicide,' Grant said, shaking his head while munching on his sandwich. 'When I commit suicide, either I'll go to the middle of a field to shoot myself or jump from a bridge. Who would like to spend their last days in the city hall haggling with an official for a reservation?' Grant snorted, almost choking on his remark that he found witty, launching tiny bits of sandwich in the air.

'Keep your mouth closed while eating!' Luna said and tried to wipe his lip to rid him of a mischievous dab of mayonnaise from his sandwich.

'How about you, love?' Grant asked while trying to chase away her hand like a pesky mosquito.

'I would probably take sleeping pills. Sounds really peaceful,' Luna said, pulling strands of her blonde hair. 'How about you, Poppy? I'd expect something more... how to put it? Hmm, flamboyant!' Luna laughed while pretending to put on airs.

'Come now!' Poppy said indignantly and crossed her arms. 'I never try to put on a show,' she puffed and took a big bite from her tuna sandwich. 'The sand- wiches are really nice, Luna! Thank you, baby. Hmm. Back to your question. I guess I might prefer hypothermia. I read that it's really peaceful and you just fall asleep, but I'm not sure. But you know I love guns, too.'

'Hello, kids. It's really nice to see you here,' Mrs. Pallas, their counselor from the school, greeted the schoolmates. She, along with her husband and teenage daughter, was now standing next to their bank in a bright red t-shirt and azure jeans in sharp contrast to her everyday gray suit at school. Saul wasn't sure whether he would have been able to recognize her without her regular clothes and tightly and tidily done French braided hair if she hadn't approached them first. But Mrs. Pallas's most striking feature was still there—her eerily long fingers that would make any piano player jealous, adorned with ten rings, resembling a spider stuck in a jewel box. Saul heartily wished indeed she would have followed a career in arts. Or simply anything else than being a counselor. Although Saul was thankful that someone steered the conversation from the macabre topic at hand, especially be- fore Grant prodded him to reveal how, not if, he planned to kill himself, Saul wasn't ecstatic to see Mrs. Pallas, either.

'Greetings, Mrs. Pallas,' Poppy replied, standing up and nodding to her family. 'We are celebrating my eighteenth birthday. Actually, we were about to cut the cake. Would you like to stay? But I wouldn't like to hold you back, either. You must have other plans with your family.'

'Happy birthday, Poppy. Congratulations,' Mrs. Pallas said, in a tone that also could have been used to console a weeping widow standing next to her husband's freshly dug grave. 'We were just heading home, so we kindly have to decline your offer. But I am glad to see you here, Saul,' Mrs. Pallas added with a smile befitting an heiress learning that her grandfather had passed away. 'It's great to see that Poppy changed your mind and brought you here. Anyway, I think we have an appointment tomorrow; I will see you then.'

'I'll see you tomorrow, Mrs. Pallas,' Saul replied with a blank expression as the counselor and her family walked away. He was thinking about how she learned

Poppy tried to bring him here. When he looked at Poppy, he saw she was blushing a bright pink color and was tugging on her hair.

'I thought we were here to eat cake. I want my cake,' Poppy said, looking away from Saul.

Luna set the chocolate angel cake on the table, and with the help of Saul, they started putting eighteen candles on it. When Luna finished, Grant passed on his lighter to Saul. By the time Saul was on the second candle, he heard a commotion rising from the other end of the park. He raised his head and saw a silhouette behind the branches walking towards them.

'Come on, keep going, or wax will drip on the cake!' Luna said to him and nudged his shoulder.

'Sorry,' Saul murmured and kept on lighting the candles. The commotion was getting nearer, and the distant silhouette behind the branches was forming into a girl. Now, he could pick up what everyone was saying.

'Next Time!'

3 more candles to go.

'Next Time!'

Then he lit the last candle.

'Next Time!'

'Come on, make a wish, Poppy!' Luna said and started to chant with their friends: 'Happy Birthday Poppy! Happy Birthday Poppy!' Then Poppy held her hair behind her head and leaned into the cake. After closing her eyes for a moment, she blew out all the candles on the first try. While Poppy accepted the congratulations, Saul was trying to make out who was coming towards them. He started shivering again and felt a disproportionate volume change in his face, hands, and even in his internal organs. Above all, his bladder was on the verge of exploding as if he had drunk liters of water before hibernating, and now was the time he rose from his slumber. Expecting that his turn was coming, he pulled the silver necklace from his pocket that he bought for Poppy.

'Next Time!'

Now Saul could see the girl that was coming towards them. She was wearing a yellow summer dress, accompanied by a red band on her arm, and seemed as if she was gliding above the grass with her bare feet. Saul couldn't help but think that with her black hair reaching almost to her waist, she looked like a giant worker bee. People on her path and those sitting on the banks were saluting her, "Next Time!" and she was, in return, waving at them and even throwing kisses to little kids.

'Is this less gruesome and more acceptable than public executions because the victim is not screaming her innocence?' Saul thought with contempt and started sweating. *'These people in the park are the offspring of the ones whose major entertainment spectacle was to gather around gallows in town squares and solemnly listen to the recited crimes: Luke for robbery, Martha for witchcraft, Hans for high treason. It was never about deterrence, was it? Even if the elderman didn't mandate people to witness it, they would have muddled around anyway, their minds clouded with bloodlust, a cry of unison in their lips: "Punish the deviant!"'*

***

'This is Sophie. This must be Sophie,' Saul said. He now knew that she was Sophie all along. Suddenly, Poppy grabbed him by the arm and turned him around.

'Am I not going to get a birthday kiss?'

Saul leaned over to kiss Poppy and felt her warm breath dissipate over his face. He once again realized that he was freezing. Not to faint on her, Saul pulled back after a small kiss and, with shaking hands, showed her the necklace that he was holding on to for dear life.

'It is really beautiful,' Poppy said with wide eyes and gave Saul another kiss. She then turned her back and gathered her hair on her chest.

Now, there were less than thirty steps between them and Sophie. He was still struggling to open the clasp of the necklace before Sophie passed by their bank. For a moment, Saul made eye contact with the girl, who returned it with a warm smile. Everyone sitting at their table, apart from him and Ezra, waved at her and said, "Next Time!"

As Sophie passed their bank and walked towards the tree, Saul felt his muscles become stiff with an unbearable tension as millions of tiny ants under his skin pulled apart and gnawed on his fibers. His best efforts to open the clasp of the necklace were to no avail.

'I can't open it. My stomach turned upside down,' Saul gulped and handed the necklace to Poppy. Then he turned towards a nearby sycamore tree and shambled towards it. Midway, Saul stopped and turned around to Sophie, who was taking the few remaining steps toward the concrete stairs.

'Sophie. No,' Saul said under his breath and took a step towards her. 'No,' he repeated louder.

'Go back to your friends,' a guard waiting by the tree said and gave Saul a tap on the shoulder.

'No!'

'Are you out of your mind, kid?'

'Sophie,' Saul screamed as the girl reached the stairs.

'This is enough,' the guard said and pushed Saul, who retaliated with a weak punch. The guard caught the punch midair and subsequently subdued Saul and called for reinforcements with a walkie-talkie: 'We have a crazy boy here. Send someone by the tree.'

After struggling for a bit, Saul realized he would not shake the guard away. Now, the ants pulling him apart started running inside his veins, sending incessant tremors throughout his body. Tears dripping from his eyes tickled his cheeks, but Saul couldn't wipe them away. Any movement, big or small, could have opened a gorge under his knees to swallow him whole. Also, unfortunately for him, there was just a single gasp of air left in the forest, and he had drawn it in a couple of seconds ago.

***

As it was the tradition in their high school to celebrate the start of their senior year, Saul's entire class had gone on a day trip to a nature reserve to have a picnic. First, they sailed close to a waterfall to glide below the rainbows, then they hiked through a nearby forest in groups of five for birdwatching. They listened to the songs of blue tits, barn swallows, and thrush nightingales. However, above all, the star of their expedition was a red-haired woodpecker.

When Sophie heard the intermittent drum roll, she immediately stopped her group and silenced them. After a couple minutes of searching, she located the bird pecking away the trunk of a pine tree and pointed to the group where to look with their binoculars.

'There. Next to the broken branch,' she said and squeezed Saul's arm. She then gave her binoculars to the boy and guided his arm to the correct angle.

'Ah! I see it now.'

'Let me also take a look,' Poppy said and squeezed herself in between Saul and Sophie by pushing away the girl. 'Show me where it is, Saul!'

'Near the broken branch,' Saul said and then leaned over to Poppy's ear. 'Are you going to pee on me next to mark your territory?' He then gave back Sophie's binoculars. 'Thank you. A really beautiful bird.'

'I was thinking of giving you a purple eye if you kept flirting with her. People would recognize that you are mine much more easily,' Poppy whispered back to Saul. 'There's also a pheasant in the tree behind,' she then called on the others to look. 'How beautiful it is! I wish I had brought my rifle with me.'

'Do you hunt?' another guy from the group then approached Poppy. 'Maybe we can go hunting together sometime.'

'I do. Usually deer and rabbits. But occasionally also birds,' she replied, then held Saul's hand. 'Thank you, but I prefer to go alone.'

'I think hunting is cruel and stupid. With all due respect,' Sophie said and pointed to a nightingale sitting atop a nearby branch.

'No one asked for your opinion,' Poppy said and took a step towards the girl. 'Besides, you can't call me stupid and say, 'With all due respect!''

'I didn't say you were stupid.'

'Calm down, girls,' Saul said and tried to pull back Poppy, but to no avail.

'Hunting is no worse than eating meat. You were with us at the BBQ last weekend. That is life. Animals are going to die, anyway.'

'So are you.'

'What the hell do you mean? Are you threatening me?' Poppy screamed back and wrestled her hand from Saul, who now stepped in front of his girlfriend.

'Do you think you're immortal?' Sophie asked and sighed as the nightingale, startled by the sudden commotion, flew away.

'Enough! Let's go back!' Saul shouted and dragged Poppy away.

***

Following a couple of hours-long excursion, they joined the rest of the amateur birdwatchers and set up campfires to prepare for an early evening dinner. While Saul was helping with cooking the meat, around the same campfire, Sophie was playing a pop song on her guitar, and everyone else was joining her to sing the chorus, 'Take me by the hand to the world's edge, I will come with you anywhere. That is my pledge.'

Poppy's head on his shoulders, flames warming his face, and surrounded by friends enjoying themselves, Saul wished for the moment to last longer. He thought of insects covered in resin, defying space-time continuity. He wanted to be like those insects, to be covered in resin, to preserve this ephemeral moment of euphoria. The archeologists who dug them up centuries later would attest to and be jealous of their joy. Alas, he knew this moment would end as any other. *'How rare it is to be aware of our good times while we are living through them,'* thought Saul. *'Sometimes years pass by, and then we reminisce about days such as this one, only to be gripped by nostalgia and regret for not laughing or enjoying them even more. As we get older, we hang on to those good memories and play them again and again on the cinema screen in front of our eyes. Our lives condensed to nothing but those rare moments that lasted maybe a couple of hours, while the rest seems like a long, miserable day. How unfortunate to live through all the pain, heartbreak, and tears to reach those sporadic oases in our lives. Unless a vagabond starts traveling in the desert again, under the smoldering sun, she does not truly appreciate the oasis she had left, as she assumes there is always one more waiting. Then, along the way, maybe miles later, she whines to herself: I wish I had rested more under those palm trees and drunk one more fist of cold water.'*

But today, Saul enjoyed one of those rare moments in life, in his personal oasis with Poppy.

Once the sun dyed the waterfalls red, the students packed their bags and marched back to their buses. Saul idled around the now deserted camp and helped the teachers put out the fires. He noticed that the girl with the guitar, Sophie, was also not heading to the bus but sitting on a nearby fallen tree trunk and strumming her guitar. Her long black hair was almost entirely covering her beautiful satin face, letting Saul only momentarily see a glimpse of her dark hazel eyes. '*Where is Ezra?*' he wondered. He had joined them for birdwatching but disappeared during the campfires. '*If he was here, I'd have encouraged him to go talk to Sophie. Who knows, maybe they would have liked each other. Maybe Ezra already knew her from some-where. He always had many friends.*'

Saul finally picked up his backpack and headed to the bus, albeit with small steps. When he glanced back, he saw that Sophie, who had left her guitar leaning on the trunk, was heading towards the waterfall. Saul, despite Poppy's pleading, refused to go near it. Whenever he looked down from a height, he always felt that a sudden urge to jump down was going to overtake him. Maybe just before they were heading back home, Sophie had overcome her own fear and wanted to peek at the orange flames gushing down to the sea. Saul now stopped walking and turned around to watch Sophie. Her head was directly fixed on a target across the waterfall that neither Saul nor anyone else around could see. He thought that when she reached the edge, she would reveal her wings like an eagle and immediately plunge down the valley below to hunt a hare she had spotted earlier.

'Come on baby, why are you idling!' Poppy shouted from the bus door and extended her hand out.

'A minute, love!' Saul answered back and turned to Sophie again, who had almost reached the waterfall.

At that moment, Saul knew she wouldn't stop.

***

'Next Time! Goodbye!' everyone around the tree shouted and waved.

When Saul looked to his left, he saw the shadow of the steel noose dangling from the branch. Without rushing, step by step, a silhouette was rising to the noose. Before the final step, the noose became a halo over the silhouette's head, momentarily blessing her as an angel. Then the halo disappeared, ostracizing her from seven heavens. Two arms appeared at the sides of the noose and then glided down. The silhouette jumped up and forward, maybe thinking she still had her angel wings. During the descent, the now miniaturized silhouette's shadow split, giving birth to another smaller one. Saul heard a big thud, followed by a smaller one.

Saul was biting his lip and tongue, trying not to scream. Once he heard the thuds, he could taste his warm, acrid blood—the taste of chocolate cake, tuna sandwich, and blood in his mouth was now too much for his stomach to handle. By the time he stopped vomiting, he was already sobbing as quietly as he could while his throbbing eyes felt like they were trying to escape their sockets. Strangely, there was still not a single gasp of air to breathe in the forest, either.

'Go home,' the guard said and pulled his knee from Saul's back

'Let's go. We should have never come here,' Ezra said and helped Saul get to his feet. 'Back off,' he said as he pushed away another guard coming close.

'Watch it, kid!'

'What happened? Are you okay?' Poppy said and rushed towards them. 'Leave him alone,' she ordered and stepped between the guards and Ezra. Before the situation escalated any further, the guard who subdued Saul pulled the others away.

'I'm sorry. I'm sorry. I ruined your birthday.' Saul said, fighting back his tears and trying to stand straight. However, there was nothing he could do to hide either his knees shaking or his face turning a bright red. 'I want to go home.'

'Let's go home together then.' Poppy said, tugging at Saul's arm.

'I beg you, please don't come.' Saul said, tears leaving a salty taste in his mouth. 'I will feel even worse if you come with us. Ezra came here by car; he will drop me home. I love you, Poppy; go back to the table, please.'

'I will not leave your side,' Poppy said, refusing his plea, and gave him a kiss on his cheek. She then locked arms with him and started walking to Ezra's car. 'It's the end of the discussion. Don't worry, love.'

***

The train stopped just outside the station. The windshield of the first wagon was covered in blood. A finger and a thumb were stuck in the grills. Passengers opened the windows and leaned from their waists to see whether the police and the cleaning crew had arrived yet. 'No one came yet,' then they informed the others in their wagon, where a communal groan rose from those inside.

'Are you okay, girl?' Theo asked the intern crouched near the pole, still vomiting her breakfast.

'Are you joking? We killed someone. I am *not* okay!'

'We didn't kill anyone,' Theo said and pulled out a pocket knife to peel an apple. 'The guy who pushed the man killed him.' He then offered the girl a slice of apple, which she didn't even acknowledge. 'We're going to be on our way soon'

'We shouldn't have speeded,' she said and looked at the front of the train with disgust and retched. 'What will we tell the police? They'll be here in minutes!'

'It has nothing to do with us!'

'You don't care because you weren't the one driving the train. You made me go faster!'

'Girl, you need to calm down,' Theo said and dragged her away from the train. 'They will ask some standard questions, and the police will be after the murderer if he isn't already caught. Besides, you wanted to drive the O-train, and you have experienced it now.'

'Are you crazy? It is not the same thing! That guy didn't want to die.'

'Tough luck,' Theo said and asked the girl to stop next to a wall providing shade from the sun. He offered the intern another slice of apple, 'It's sour, so it will stop you from vomiting.' At first hesitant, the girl moved this time and took the slice, which she swallowed after two bites. Theo then pulled out a handkerchief and wiped his face. 'Not everyone who wants to live can. It used to be that not everyone who wanted to die couldn't, either. Do you see the factory there with the orange roof?'

'I do,' the girl nodded and sat down.

'My father used to work there as a welder. Grueling, back-breaking work with no time off, for laughable pay.' He then cut another slice for the girl, who accepted it without a fuss this time. The apple did help her. 'One day, another welder in my father's shift made a mistake and ruined a part. The bosses punished him by withholding his weekly salary. The guy then jumped from the top floor right on top of the punch clock machines. Shortly after that, it turned into an epidemic. Every day after, a young man jumped from the top floor.'

'How did they stop it?' the intern asked and stood up at once when she saw the approaching police car in the distance. Theo's words had calmed her. She was just an intern, after all. The police would understand.

'They built a net on every floor and locked the windows so people couldn't kill themselves.'

'Did it stop the people?'

'It did. At least during the work hours inside the factory.'

'I guess paying them a good salary and giving decent breaks wasn't an option. You're right. A unionized job doesn't sound bad after all.'

***

'Looks terrible,' said the young police officer, kneeling by the front of the wagon and looking at the parts and bits stuck on the grills.

'It does. At least the guy didn't suffer for long,' Theo said and turned to the police sergeant beside him. 'Did you catch the killer?'

'No need to. He turned himself in.'

'He deserves a death sentence,' the intern stamped her foot on the ground but started retching and immediately turned her back to the train again. 'He killed an innocent man,' she said and tried to stop vomiting.

'It was a mistake to abolish it,' Theo said and wiped his head again with the crumpled handkerchief.

'We are not a delusional god who decides when a person dies or lives,' the police sergeant said and called over the young officer. 'However, I can assure you that justice will be served. To anyone who was involved.'

'What does that mean?'

'You two were driving the train, I assume.'

'I was the only one driving it,' Theo said, and the wide-eyed intern looked over her shoulder at him. 'She's just an intern. Why?'

'Eyewitnesses claim you were going over the speed limit through the platform.'

'I don't think so.'

'Well, we need to ask you to come with us to the station for questioning.'

'What the hell does that mean?' Theo said, shaking his fist and taking a step towards the sergeant, startling the young officer who put his hands on his hips. 'Am I under arrest?'

'If you want to put it that way, sure. But I would just see it as an invitation for questioning.'

'What a damn day!' Theo then threw the core of the apple towards the train.

Part 2

To be, or not to be, that is the question:
Whether 'tis nobler in the mind to suffer
The slings and arrows of outrageous fortune,
Or to take arms against a sea of troubles
And by opposing end them. To die—to sleep,

— William Shakespeare, *Hamlet*, Act 3, Scene 1

The altercation with the guard left a bruise on Saul's left cheekbone, and once his dad asked what happened, he didn't lie, despite knowing too well it would result in an earful. Which it did. But he didn't want to budge anymore.

He went to bed early, and through his nightmare, he wrestled with Sophie's vision, asking, 'Why didn't you save me, Saul?' But every time he tried to reach her, a multitude of apparitions pinned him on the ground. 'Why Sophie?' he bellowed while trying to get away from the apparitions, 'Don't do it!' He woke up screaming and drenched in sweat. Then went back to sleep to try to fail to save her once more.

***

With the first rays of the sun, he entered the school building and headed towards a classroom in the basement for the third meeting with other people opposing the referendum–a meager dozen citizens who connected with each other through noticeboards and word of mouth, trying to build a political campaign. Through the small window in the door, Saul saw Francis moving up and down by the blackboard, scribbling sentences and erasing others. The thirty-year-old Francis had become the leader of their group, as they deemed him the most experienced to run a political campaign based on his experience as a telemarketer. What he lacked in stature, he made up for in energy, stemming from the thrill of being an underdog in this race and finding meaning to his life.

'Come on in, Saul. We're going over finalizing our slogan,' Francis called the boy in. 'Ladies and gents, our time is running out. Do we all agree on the "Right to Love. Vote for No"?'

'Sounds a bit off. Doesn't rhyme,' Saul said and took a seat in the front row. He took a deep breath and closed his eyes. Since yesterday, he had been oscillating between suddenly screaming and falling into an anger fit or cowering in a corner and crying his eyes out. He wanted to run away, as he felt all the four walls of the classroom closing on him. 'We have to stop this,' he murmured to himself and squeezed his knees. 'We have to.'

'I agree with the boy,' Micah, a retired police chief, said. He had the constant, weary look on his face as a relic of the transition from a profession in which people listened to his orders to being another civilian without any meaningful power. 'What if they counter with "If you love someone, let them go"?'

'Are you going to keep shooting down ideas or come up with something?' Francis said and threw the chalk to the floor. He then walked behind the teacher's desk and took a couple of deep breaths. 'Sorry. I'm just... just. We are. You know,' he then pointed at the people sitting in the classroom. 'We have to find something and start distributing the pamphlets. We are behind our plan. We have to save people.'

'I know, I know. No worries,' Micah said, leaning back in his chair and lit up a cigarette.

'They don't allow...' a woman sitting behind tried to ask Micah to put down his cigarette, but the man waved and stopped her.

'I couldn't help much in the past. I can't help more now, either. But I have to tell the truth. We can't keep lying to ourselves. Who read a pamphlet in his or her life and changed their opinion? Anyone?' Micah then turned around and looked around the classroom, where no one reacted. 'That's what I thought too,' then he exhaled the smoke and coughed in his elbow.

'We also get a slot at the TV debate,' Saul said without raising his head from looking at his shoes.

'I know. But we are stuck with the village idiot parliament representative who said we should go back to the old days and drag people who had committed suicide through the streets.'

'What's your suggestion then, Micah?' Francis asked, leaning his back on the wall and crossing his arms on his chest. 'Do nothing? Let people die?'

'I buried my son last week,' Micah said and drew a big breath from his cigarette, whose tip burned a bright red again. 'I have nothing, to be honest. I couldn't even change his mind. My son. Sometimes, I think the referendum can be for the better. It would take the guilt off our chests. I wasn't allowed to interfere, so I couldn't do anything,' he said and threw the butt of the cigarette on the floor and put it out with his foot. 'But I still want to help people and you. Those who still have someone to lose. I think we foremost lack publicity. People are not aware of our existence. Our arguments. Whatever they are. They don't think for themselves either,' Micah said and rose from his chair. 'We need to be in the newspapers. Something newsworthy. I want to give you a final boost,' he said and drew a gun from under his jacket. A couple of women screamed, Francis froze in his place, his eyes wide, and another guy took a step towards Micah.

'Put the gun down!'

'How ironic will it be?' Micah then pointed the gun under his chin.

***

Despite waiting for the police and the ambulance, Saul arrived on time at the counselor's office. If he was even a minute late, he would have endured a rant about being responsible and punctual: 'The world does not revolve around you, Saul. You can't disrespect me, Saul. Do you think you are so important that everyone needs to wait for you, Saul?' He was never in the mood for a rant, so he was always on time, including that day. He doubted if Mrs. Pallas would have accepted the excuse that his morning meeting had taken a different turn than originally planned.

Other than that, he wanted to be on the good side of Mrs. Pallas, as she was the one sending out the university applications with her approval. Falling out of her favor would have undesirable consequences. '*So, let's get in and out,*' thought Saul, '*and be done with this as quickly and painlessly as possible.*' He tried to push Micah and Sophie out of his mind. If possible, for an hour at least. There was going to be enough time to grieve and think. There always was.

Mrs. Pallas's door was already open, but he still knocked.

'Good morning. Can I come in?'

'Take a seat, Saul, ' Mrs. Pallas, locking eyes with him, pointed to the wooden chair across her desk. Saul always found Mrs. Pallas's room eerie and disturbing. Today, he thought he knew why. Last week in physics class, they learned that one of the fundamental forces in nature is entropy, which dictates that everything in the universe is in a constant, gradual descent into disorder. Apart from Mrs. Pallas's room, of course. It seemed with every passing second, the room was getting more organized by an invisible hand. For months, Saul had been visiting Mrs. Pallas' room weekly but never saw a paperclip out of place, a single sheet of paper disoriented on the table, or a pen out of the holder away from its brethren. God knows why or how, but even all the books on her shelf were the same height. He chuckled when he imagined Mrs. Pallas going to a bookstore with a ruler and asking the librarians in which section the fifteen centimeters books were.

'You seem to be in a good mood, Saul. I am happy to see that,' Mrs. Pallas spoke, wearing the facial expression of an old lover congratulating a newlywed couple.

'It's my favorite time of the week, as always. I'm saddened to see that this will be our last meeting.'

'Why are you under the impression that this will be our last meeting, Saul?' Mrs. Pallas smirked and crossed her fingers, displaying the ring on each one.

'I started coming here because I had saved Sophie from jumping off the cliff.' Saul said, reclining slightly in the wooden chair. 'As Sophie is now… gone, I don't think we need to meet any more. Do you know that she had committed suicide yesterday?' Shadows from yesterday's picnic were still etched on Saul's iris. Also, mentioning Sophie's name started churning his stomach again. But he knew he had to conceal any emotion from Mrs. Pallas if he hoped to end these weekly torture sessions.

'Of course, I do know about Ms. Sophie's decision,' Mrs. Pallas replied with a slight indignation in her voice and crossed her arms. 'As for our meetings… I will be the one deciding on that,' the counselor said, pressing her lips into a thin, straight line. 'We will get back to that later. But I am admittedly happy that I saw you yesterday in the park. I take it as a point of improvement that our meetings aren't for nothing.' Then she stood up from her chair, gently pushed it back under the table, and walked to the bookshelf. Saul was not sure how witnessing the suicide of a friend counted as an improvement point, but he had learned to keep his thoughts to himself after a couple of meetings.

'Poppy is now also able to vote this year. So, you can take part in the historic referendum together. It will be a great honor for our generation.'

'Seems so.'

'We will vote in unison to show how irradicated sense of freedom is in our communities across the land.'

'True show of democracy.'

Mrs. Pallas turned back to look at Saul to see whether he was mocking her or at least showing enough decency to veil it so she could ignore his insolence.

'Do you know the history of Farewell Tree?' Mrs. Pallas asked, now holding a bright red book in her hand.

'I know the city restored the tree after the revolution to its purpose today.'

'I am talking about its history. Its origin.'

'I am afraid not,' Saul replied and shook his head. The last thing he wanted to learn now was more about that cursed tree, but apparently, Mrs. Pallas had a different idea. He felt his heart filling with rage at Mrs. Pallas's indifference to Sophie. *'Thirty more minutes, then I am out. I do not need to see her again.'* Saul thought, so he started taking deep breaths.

'In that case, I would like you to read pages forty to forty-three from this book, and we can discuss it,' Mrs. Pallas said, giving Saul the book and returning to her table.

'Do you want me to read it for next week?' Saul asked with disbelief that he was going to need to come here next week as well.

'No. It is a quick read. You can finish it now, then we discuss it,' Mrs. Pallas said and lowered her head to papers that looked like university applications.

Saul read the title of the book *"Celebrating Fifty Years of Freedom"* written by Helen Pallas. He then turned to the bookshelf and realized they were all written by her. 'That explains why they are all the same size.' Saul murmured.

'I do not have all day, Saul. I have appointments with other students. Start reading please!' Mrs. Pallas said without lifting her head up from the application in her hand. A rejection.

So, Saul flipped to page forty and started reading.

***

Even though initially the detractors had slandered the Individual Freedom Philosophy as a mere financially driven agenda to reduce the burden on hospitals, prisons, and state welfare system by encouraging people to end their lives earlier than their potential natural course after the Great War the philosophy consequently managed to promulgate over the land. With Individual Freedom Philosophy's near-unanimous adoption in society, groundbreaking changes necessitated by a modern way of life came to fruition through improvements in every aspect of our existence, ranging from updated school curriculums to revised urban planning practices.

During the years of repression of individuality and freedom by the state and society at large, successive despotic governments castrated the Farewell Tree from its purpose. They removed the steel noose, which today is the beloved symbol of our city. Then, eventually, as a crowning achievement to mark our arduous liberation, the time had come to restore the Farewell Tree to its celebrated origins.

At this point, as there are multiple accounts of the origin story, some of which are solely created to smear the Farewell Tree and what it stands for, we would like to diverge to reiterate its true inception:

Jus Primae Noctis, a Latin phrase meaning "right of the first night," was a concession given to kings, feudal lords, or other aristocratic rulers to have sexual relations, almost exclusively with the bride, on her wedding night. However, in most cases, the ruler class did not exercise their legal right to earn their serf's favor to prevent a potential uprising, etc. Instead, they either requested a payment as a tax or a share from the bride's dowry or outright waived it as a gift to the newlywed couple.

However, historical records from the ducal archive and local tales around the early fifteenth century note that a newly appointed vassal to our city, which used to be a fiefdom at the time, refused to waive or monetize the concession, insisting on a newlywed bride to be with him during the wedding night.

Despite the refusal of the groom, at the end of the wedding, the vassal's men transferred the bride to the castle. Although the convention had dictated that after the first night, the vassal should return the bride to her husband, the ruler declined to follow the unwritten law. Feeling indignant about what he saw as a usurpation, the groom visited the castle the next night and demanded his wife back. However, he was told that the vassal had declared their marriage null, and he had married the girl himself. As the serf, who chronicles write to be a skilled blacksmith, reasoned that it was not possible to overpower guards on his own, he sought help from other subjects of the fiefdom. Alas, fearing retribution and probably thinking that once the vassal was married, he would not bother other families, no other villager helped the young blacksmith.

The next day, while the young groom was still planning for a way to get back his ex-bride, the vassal's guards knocked on his door with an order: forge a new wedding sword for the ruler as a gift. Enraged by the request, which the blacksmith saw as insolent, he refused to comply.

Upon hearing that his order was declined, the vassal declared that one house every night would be set ablaze in the village until the young blacksmith obeyed the order and started forging the gift. When the villagers heard the decree, they gathered in front of the blacksmith's family home and begged him to forge the sword. Instead, the blacksmith asked them to help him to storm the castle and get his wife back. Unfortunately for the young guy, the villagers declined his plan. One of them even went as far as offering his daughter as a new bride for the blacksmith instead if the young man agreed to comply with the vassal's wish.

After the first night, the vassal's soldiers burnt down one of the farmers' houses and visited the blacksmith again: if he refused to start forging the sword, his parents would be sent to the dungeon (which is now a popular tourist attraction in our city), and if that did not work, he would receive a finger of his previous wife every night, until none was left. The blacksmith sent the messengers away, declaring that he would forge a gift for the vassal.

The next morning, villagers found the body and severed head of the blacksmith by the tree in the main square, under the steel noose he had forged, with a note nailed to the trunk of the tree:

'You do not have any power over me now.'

***

Saul lifted his head from the book with a thousand questions swirling inside his head like a school of anchovies swimming away from hungry dolphins. 'I read the part,' Saul said, closed the book, and placed it on Mrs. Pallas's desk.

'What do you think, Saul?' Mrs. Pallas asked, stamping the application in her hand and neatly placing it on top of the others piled on her desk. Another rejection.

'I am confused as to why villagers so easily submitted to the requests of the vassal even though he burned one of their houses.' Saul said without hesitating. He thought that if he said he didn't have any questions, Mrs. Pallas was going to bombard him with her own and steer the conversation to a point she had planned well in advance. But now he wished he had gone with another neutral question to deflect from the story. Such as, 'How a young blacksmith in medieval ages learned to read and write.'

'What do you think they should have done, Saul? Grab their pitchforks and confront the vassal's men?' Mrs. Pallas said with a narrow grin.

'I am not sure,' Saul said, slightly blushing. 'But submitting to the vassal's request definitely would not be an option. That would only embolden him further. He would want more taxes or more work. I don't know,' he continued, slightly stuttering and yet still trying to control the trembling in his voice. He knew he hadn't thought his answer through, and he was getting angrier by the minute.

'Let's do a thought experiment,' Mrs. Pallas said and leaned back in her rotating chair. Saul had never seen her getting this comfortable. He wished he'd said he didn't have any questions. 'First case, you grab your pitchforks, and you are killed by the vassal's men. Who is now going to look after your own family?' Mrs. Pallas asked. When Saul attempted to answer her, she waved and cut him off. Saul then resigned to his fate and bit his tongue. The second option is you manage to kill the vassal. What would happen then? The king would send an army to squash the uprising. So, the endgame for the farmers must be to overthrow the monarchy and establish democracy,' Mrs. Pallas said and now shifted to the front, placed her elbows on the desk, and put her chin on her clenched fists.

'Well, at some point, someone exactly did that,' Saul said. 'I don't see any kings around here, do you?'

'That is true,' Mrs. Pallas said, still smiling. 'It is such a shame that there was not a hero like you back then.' the counselor said and flung her arms open, laughing. 'You would have saved the blacksmith like you did Sophie.' Now, she was not smiling and locked her eyes on Saul. 'You have said that you had saved Ms. Sophie. Tell me now, Saul. What did you save her from?'

'From jumping off the cliff,' Saul said, trying to keep his voice from rising. Now he was sitting on the edge of his chair, like a cat readying to pounce on a mouse.

'That is not what I am asking. Why had she decided to do so?' she shook her head, leaned back in her chair, and crossed her fingers to display the rings on her spider hands. Saul did not give an answer and kept looking at her, slightly feeling dizzy. 'You don't know because you didn't even ask her. Ms. Sophie was also visiting me regularly. Did you know how she felt about you saving her?' the counselor asked further with a big smirk on her face that she did not even try to hide. 'This is why the referendum really matters, Saul. You can't go out and about to ruin other people's lives and plans without repercussions.'

Saul, indeed, had never asked Sophie why she tried to jump off from the cliff. After he stopped her that day, Saul and Ezra sat next to her on the bus while Sophie shed muted tears. Then they walked her home on a long, silent night. Neither Saul nor Ezra wanted to broach the subject, as they did not know what to say. When Saul and Ezra left her home, they sufficed with a goodbye and gave her a lopsided hug. In the following days, Saul only saw Sophie in the corridor of their school, where she always threw him a smile. Saul always interpreted it as a sign of gratitude. He always thought Sophie's decision to walk towards the cliff was nothing but a bout of hysteria. He could now clearly see that he was pretending so as not to shoulder a heavy burden he did not feel ready to lift. Saul was now wondering what Sophie had gone through, as everyone in their class witnessed what had happened. 'Did they shun her? Make fun of her?' And above all, the burning question inside his heart: 'Why did Sophie kill herself?' His rage subsided as quickly as it built up, leaving behind a feeling of piercing regret and a bunch of 'could have beens' and 'would have beens.'

'Aren't you going to say something, Saul?' Mrs. Pallas asked, but now her smile was also gone.

'No,' Saul shook his head and searched the tiled floor for some answers that might have dropped from his pocket.

'Look at me, Saul,' Mrs. Pallas said, then stood up from her chair. She walked to the front of her table and sat on its edge. Saul caught a glimpse of his miserable self in her rings; he was caught in an amber prison with his own reflections. 'As you seem really distraught now, we are going to continue our discussion next week. Keep in mind that my aim is not to torture you or anyone else for that matter,' Mrs. Pallas said.

'Why are you doing this, then?'

'To prevent further suffering for you and anyone else,' the counselor said. 'When I was twelve, I found out that my father hanged himself in our living room. He also left us a note.' Saul locked his eyes to hers to see an emotion he could connect with. But she carried on as if to explain a particularly terrible day at the beach when she overslept and got sunburnt. 'This and that, he can't take it anymore and that he is a burden to us. All nonsense, you know.' She shrugged and waved her hand as if to chase out a pesky fly. 'You can't expect people to pinpoint the cause of their suffering every time. It was hard for me initially,' she said and momentarily focused on the bookshelf. 'But in the end, I was happy that he didn't suffer further.'

Saul looked back to Mrs. Pallas's face, which was contorted to an expression meant to display compassion from her pressed lips, forming a coy smile, to the squinting of her eyes. But something wasn't quite right in his eyes.

'I have to warn you, If I do not see a rapid improvement in the last two months we have, I cannot approve your college applications,' Mrs. Pallas said in a soft, tiger-like purring tone. 'However, all is not lost. I am happy that Poppy talked some sense into you to go to the park. You are lucky to have her.'

'What does this have to do with Poppy? I don't understand!'

'I thought Poppy told you. I think then you should talk to her.' Mrs. Pallas stopped him. 'Our appointment is over. Don't be late to your class,' and pointed to the door, displaying the amber prison where Saul had resided.

'She knew Sophie was going to come to the tree then. You told her!' Saul said and rose from his chair, hands clenched into fists. 'You asked her to drag me to witness Sophie killing herself.' Saul then remembered when she said that it was great that Poppy brought him here and the face of her girlfriend blushing.

'I arranged nothing but only deduced that there is a coincidence that I should take advantage of, for your sake,' the counselor said as she crossed her arms over her chest and walked back to her chair.

'My sake? I call that bullshit!' Saul said and pointed his finger at Mrs. Pallas.

'Out of my room at once, Saul!' Mrs. Pallas said, turning around. 'Come back when you know how to behave yourself.'

Saul heard the commotion of students who were starting to move to their next class in the corridors. Then, a student knocked on Mrs. Pallas's door and asked for permission to come in.

The knock brought Saul back to his senses, and he left the room at once to find Poppy.

***

Saul flung the classroom door open and walked into the 'Suicide Philosophy' class, suddenly drawing all eyes to him. But after a momentary pause, the commotion rolled on again, with students huddled in small groups gossiping about friends while a couple of studious ones went over their homework before handing it in. Poppy was nowhere to be found. He then walked over to her friend's desk.

'Where's Poppy?'

'Good morning to you too, Saul,' the girl laughed at Saul's boorishness. The girl with the ponytail had a big nose that ill-suited her face but simultaneously provided a unique charm. 'Poppy didn't come to school today. I haven't seen her.'

'Take your seats and pass over your papers,' Mr. Lewis, the philosophy teacher, said as soon as he entered the classroom and headed towards his desk with brisk steps, ending the commotion and dispersing the huddled groups at once. He was a handsome, stocky man in his late thirties with a face made up of soft features accompanied by a feminine jawline, contrasting the air of ruggedness he cast forth. After he put down his book, he picked up a chalk and loosened his tight blue tie that matched elegantly with his navy blue suit. Girls in the classroom who became

women in the past summer started to find Mr. Lewis's class more and more interesting every day.

Mr. Lewis then pointed to one of the students sitting near the door.

'Robert, please go to the chemistry lab and ask for the cart.'

Although Robert clearly was confused about why he was going to the chemistry
lab for the philosophy class, he quickly leaped to his feet and headed for it.

The student who collected the homework from the pupils put the papers on
the teacher's desk. Mr. Lewis walked back, grabbed the paper on top of the pile,
and glanced over it quickly:

'Homer's *Iliad* is an exemplar for the view of suicide in primitive societies,' Mr.
Lewis said with a grin on his face as he read the paper in his large hands. He then
lifted his head to scan the class and groaned, 'On a side note, I hope other papers
are not littered with simple grammar errors like this one. Do I need to go over the
difference between *effect* and *affect* again?' Saul saw one girl blush by the window.

Their homework was to read and analyze Homer's *Iliad* to tell why readers
throughout centuries didn't embrace Achilles' death as a suicide while another
great soldier, Ajax's death, did. Saul didn't enjoy this class a bit, as he found it
grim, but at least he had enjoyed the reading this week. He had an inexplicable
pleasure from reading the convoluted machinations, divine interventions, and the
sacrosanctity of honor, even during the wars in ancient times. On top of that,
knowing that it was all true, apart from the regular visit of deities, of course, that
happened at some point in time, palpitated his imagination even more. Mrs. Pallas
told Saul that he had to pass this class with perfect scores if he was supposed to
have a sliver of hope to get a good recommendation. So, Saul was listening with
his full attention.

'Achilles's death was foretold by his mother, Thetis, a clairvoyant. You and I
might not believe in clairvoyants, but Achilles took his mother's prophecy by heart.
He knew if he were to join the Trojan war, he would gain great fame and honor
but alas perish at a young age.' Mr. Lewis said while fidgeting with the chalk and
dusting his palm and fingers. He then started pacing inside the classroom from
door to windows without rushing and throwing stern glances to make sure he had
everyone's attention. He needed not to worry, as boys were interested in the story
of warriors, while girls enjoyed watching him relentlessly anyway.

'If someone commits an act to end his life, without coercion, that is suicide. While it is true that most people commit suicide to seek refuge from worldly worries, honor, or anger, there are various other reasons. Achilles, for instance, valued ever ephemeral life less than eternal glory.'

A scrawny ginger boy sitting in the front row raised his hand;

'Sir, you mentioned that suicide needs to be without coercion. In that case, warrior Ajax's death might not be classified as suicide. His judgment was clouded by the goddess Athena, even though he slew himself.'

'That is the discussion I want to read in these papers.' Mr. Lewis said. 'Our topic today is suicide safety.'

Robert then rolled inside with an open wooden cart and pushed it up to the teacher's desk. The cart had two plastic bottles labeled alcohol, a pair of Bunsen burners, and a black leather briefcase.

'Since 1920, after the Great War and the rapid acceptance of Freedom Doctrine, suicide has been on the first five of death causes,' Mr. Lewis said and then turned to the blackboard to start a list. 'Who will tell me what is the first death cause?'

'Cancer?' the scrawny ginger boy said.

'No. Any more guesses?'

'Heart attack,' one of the girls by the window guessed.

'Yes. Correct. Heart attack is part of an umbrella term called "Ischemic heart disease," and it is indeed the leading cause of death,' the teacher said and wrote it as the first item. He had very nice handwriting that would make a calligrapher jealous. Saul once heard that it is possible to reveal someone's personality through their writing. 'I wish I knew how to do it. I wonder what I can deduce for Mr. Lewis.'

The second item I will write myself, "Cerebrovascular disease," which includes stroke and aneurysms caused by vascular failure. What is the third item?'

'Suicide!' one student from the back row chimed in.

'Correct. Number four is Accidents, and number five is Cancer.'

'How about euthanasia?'

'We, of course, consider it part of suicide. The city doesn't track it separately.'

After he completed the list, Mr. Lewis turned back to the cart and started placing the items on the cart on his desk. 'It's getting hot in here, and we are going to fire up the burners shortly, which I feel won't help the problem.' The teacher pointed to the students to open the window. He then walked to the door to leave it ajar. When the student pried open the windows, a sudden yet mellow gust of cicada and nightingale opera rushed in to fill the room. Saul felt they were scolding him for sitting in the classroom wasting his time, and was tempted to join them. '*How nice it would have been to sit on the grass outside with my head on Poppy's lap,*' he thought. Even now, when he took a deep breath, he almost drew in her light honey-infused perfume. He imagined resting on Poppy's lap, locking his eyes on her lower pink lip, ever twitching slowly, while her tidily cut blue nails scratched his skull to unearth a spring of warmth encompassing his entire body. He never felt so awake yet drowsy, waking up in a dream while sleeping away at night. 'Why did you let Sophie die, Poppy? Tell me?' he would have murmured to Poppy while running his fingers through her hair.

'*Why did Poppy do this to me? Why did Poppy do this to Sophie?*' Saul thought. As the tide of anger ebbed, what was left were the ruins of sand castles made up of disappointment and scruples that once stood high as idols of fidelity and passion.

'What is the most common suicide method?' Mr. Lewis asked while setting up the Bunsen burners and opening the briefcase.

'Hanging!'

'Correct! For both males and females, hanging is the most common form of self-inflicted suicide. Meaning if we don't consider euthanasia. For males, the following two methods are firearms and poisoning, with various liquids or gasses such as carbon monoxide, and for females, poisoning and jumping.' When Mr. Lewis finished his sentence, he drew a Damascus steel paring knife with a wooden handle from the briefcase. Now, the classroom fell silent as the teacher started slowly pacing the classroom.

'It is imperative that you are aware of the consequences of your suicide choice if you ever decide to end your life one day.' Mr. Lewis said while flipping the knife in his hand back and forth. Sun glistened on the Damascus steel, which had a pattern of a rocky sea at the height of a typhoon. Saul felt the blade hypnotized him; he was a fisherman getting drawn into the eye of the storm.

'For example, let's take jumping off a bridge or cliff into a large body of water beneath us. Almost certainly, the person would die upon impact,' Mr. Lewis said and stopped to look around the classroom to enjoy the full attention of the class. Then he started walking back among the students towards his desk. 'However, a certain amount of people would only break their bones and not sustain any fatal injuries. What would happen in that case?' Mr. Lewis asked and scanned the class. A couple of kids raised their hands, but Mr. Lewis wanted to hear from someone else:

'Tell me, Saul. What would happen to them?'

'They would surface and try to get to the shore to try again one more time,' Saul said, followed by an eruption of laughter from the class, breaking the tension, as he was determined not to let Mr. Lewis enjoy his lecture.

'First, come here, Saul, and help me set up the burners. Secondly, most probably, they can't. Upon impact, if they break their limbs, they can't surface, so they would drown and get eaten by crabs and fish. Imagine that you've changed your mind, and suddenly you're drowning, attacked by fish, unable to do anything.' Mr. Lewis said and then turned on one of the burners, which shot a wild blue flame up in the air.

'Do you know how to sterilize the blades, Saul?'

'Wipe them with alcohol and run them through the burner?'

'You would only burn yourself that way, as the alcohol would ignite,' the teacher said with a grin, triggering laughter from the other pupils, this time at Saul's expense. 'Run the blade through the open fire, then disinfect with the alcohol.' Mr. Lewis said and then handed the knife to his pupil.

'Sometimes, in their nets, fishermen would catch the corpse of a person who jumped from a bridge. You would recognize whether they had drowned from the mucus froth formation around their nose.' The teacher said, pointing to his nose and walking towards the windows to look outside. While holding the knife over the open flame, Saul was keeping an eye on his teacher. It was obvious to him that Mr. Lewis's dramatic pauses and turns were well planned in advance to impress the classroom. 'Even if they made it to the shore as Saul suggests,' Mr. Lewis continued and gestured towards his pupil without turning away from the window, 'during the winter months, the unfortunate individual would suffer from hypothermia, which is not a quick, painless way to go either.'

Mr. Lewis then started to take off his jacket. Everyone in the classroom was now holding their breaths, eyes locked on the teacher. 'As I said, the aim of this class is to provide you with the necessary tools to make informed decisions on terms of suicide both from a philosophical and practical aspect,' Mr. Lewis continued.

Saul had held the knife to open the fire as much as his fingers permitted him to touch the tang. While Mr. Lewis started walking back to his desk, Saul was still waving the knife, trying to cool it down. The teacher placed his jacket on the back of the chair, unbuttoned the sleeves of his shirt, and started rolling them up.

'Another popular suicide method is cutting one's own wrists. It is again a torturously slow method with a low chance of success.' Mr. Lewis warned the classroom and finished rolling his sleeves. His muscular forearms were riddled with horizontal cuts on both sides. The cuts made it apparent that this wasn't the first time he was putting on a show. Saul poured the alcohol on the knife and wiped it down with the tissues he found in the briefcase. Mr. Lewis asked Saul to hand him over the knife. When Saul tried to pass over the knife by holding out the blade, Mr. Lewis mocked him, 'Always hand over a knife by the handle; otherwise, someone might cut themselves,' and winked at his pupil.

Mr. Lewis then turned to the classroom. 'When you cut your wrists shallowly and horizontally, blood will soon clog the veins. So, you would always need to cut vertically and deep along the veins. However, if you cut too deep, then you would damage your tendons, meaning you can't use your fingers to cut your other wrist.' Saul felt a mix of disgust and anger piling inside him. '*Is this show really necessary?*'

Mr. Lewis first lifted the knife in his right hand in the air up to his shoulder, then lowered it to his left arm that stood parallel to the ground and made a horizontal shallow cut. Blood immediately started slowly trickling down to the sides. Saul had focused on Mr. Lewis's face, which did not drop the smile he'd owned since the beginning of the class, even for a moment, without a trace of pain. 'Blood flow will stop in a couple of minutes,' Mr. Lewis assured the class, enjoying the peak attention he garnered. 'And if Saul has sterilized the knife well, I have nothing else to fear.' He then chuckled along with the rest of the class. 'Cutting the wrists is more of a way of self-harming than suicide. Its causes can range from seeking an adrenaline rush rooted in a perceived guilty pleasure to an unhealthy coping mechanism with stress. I want to take away the mystery and allure behind it.' Mr. Lewis then walked back to his desk and pressed a gauze on his wrist.

'There are extra knives inside the briefcase. Feel free to try it yourself to see that this is not an ideal way to end your life. Be careful not to create a mess, and clean the knives thoroughly before putting them back in the briefcase.' Eager students formed a line before the Bunsen burners to try the stunt themselves. Saul, not willing to cut himself, left the burners on and returned to his desk.

'You will have new homework in three weeks: Aristoteles argued that committing suicide is not fair for the state as the individual would then shirk his responsibilities and duties. In that case, please discuss whether an individual would be in his right to end his life if the state fails to uphold its own end of the bargain. Or would ever an individual be able to pay their debts to the society and state to gain the right to control his existence?' Mr. Lewis said and wrote the assignment on the blackboard while his arm was still bleeding, in a visibly smaller quantity, through the gauze. 'It will be three pages.'

A collective groan rose from the class; 'We have Physics homework also due in two weeks!'

'Three and a half pages. Any more objections?' Mr. Lewis said and, content with the silence, shook his head. He then walked over to Saul's desk. 'Are not you going to try it yourself?'

'Do I have to? Is not this a free city?' Saul smirked, hiding his frustration and anger at what he saw as a masquerade.

'Absolutely not. You are free to choose your own method once you feel the time is right. I just want you to be aware of the options.'

Part 3

But at the bottom, the immanent philosopher sees in the entire universe only the deepest longing for absolute annihilation, and it is as if he clearly hears the call that permeates all spheres of heaven: Redemption! Redemption! Death to our life! and the comforting answer: you will all find annihilation and be redeemed!

— Philipp Mainländer, *The Philosophy of Salvation*

Saul was lying on his bed, staring at the ceiling covered with reflective stars and planets that his mother had put there when he was little to ease his fear of darkness. His father would mock him when Saul was little and say, 'You are a man. Men aren't afraid of the dark. Perhaps you're a little girl.' Saul would get angry, stomp his foot, and shake his fist: 'I'm not a little girl. I'm not afraid of the dark.' But once the night descended, and stars were still absent from his ceiling, darkness petrified him. Some nights, especially if there was a thunderstorm, his little heartbeat would challenge a rabbit chased by the lord's hounds. On those nights, he would sneak to his older sister's bed, where she would be already waiting for him. He knew his sister would not have sent him away or reprimanded him as his dad would. He would jump immediately onto his sister's bosom and bury his face on her chest, drowning in lilac-infused warmth, covered under her curly black hair. She, in turn, would hold him tight in her embrace and kiss him on the crown of his head.

'You can sleep with me tonight.'

'My dad is right. I'm a coward. I'm afraid of the dark.'

'Let me tell you something, Saul. Being brave is not being fearless at all. It's acting despite your fears. You managed to hop off your bed, walk in the dark corridors, and come to me.'

'But I still can't sleep on my own.'

'Don't worry; we all get braver eventually. I promise.'

He missed her deeply. For the fourth time, he was going to visit her grave on her birthday, which coincided with the annual celebration of the re-opening of the

Farewell Tree at noon, along with his mother and Ezra to bring his sister her favorite blue flowers. 'Happy Birthday.'

Saul rolled to his side. Briefly, he thought about going to Poppy's house after school, but he knew he had to calm down before facing her. '*What am I going to do anyway if I lose my temper before her parents? Anyway, tomorrow, I'll see her at the zoo.*' They would have more than enough time to talk there. '*Maybe it was for the better that I didn't find her right away in the classroom. Did she not come to the school on purpose?*'

'*Mrs. Pallas had a point,*' he thought to himself. '*I never asked Sophie why she had attempted to jump off the cliff.*' He shuddered at the thought of her meeting the fate described by Mr. Lewis: broken legs and arms, helplessly drowning in the icy waters. '*Maybe if she took Mr. Lewis's class, she might not have even attempted to jump there, and I would have never got involved in the first place,*' he chuckled to himself. What was he involved in? Even though it was a bitter pill to swallow, maybe he was really an intruder, condemning Sophie to many more months of agony until she mustered the courage to end it all again. He rolled in the bed once more. '*If I could turn back the clock to that accursed day, was I now going to let Sophie jump, get on the bus, and go on with my day as if nothing happened? What bothered Sophie then couldn't have been a moment of rashness; she wasn't there out of the blue to stroll through the park. Rather than turning the clock back and letting Sophie fly off the cliff,*' he thought, '*I should have asked what bothered her.*' Maybe, indeed, he was afraid to shoulder a burden. '*But then what if she had an incurable, agonizing disease? Was I going to say sorry, steal my dad's car, and drive Sophie to the cliff the next day myself?*' He rolled over again.

***

A knock on the door interrupted Saul's thoughts.

'Dinner is almost ready. Wash your hands and set the table, please, baby,' Saul's mother said and barged in without waiting for his permission.

'Knocking is no help if you aren't going to wait for me to say, "Come in"' Saul protested without rising from bed but shifting to sitting.

'Am I a vampire?'

'What are you talking about?'

Saul's Mother, Margaret, though her friends always preferred calling her Daisy, threw her head back and had a hearty laugh. *'I can't remember the last time I saw her laughing,'* thought Saul. Although Daisy was a petite woman in her late forties who worked as a nurse in a children's hospital, she could have passed by for a young mother in her mid-thirties. Her loosely gathered wavy chocolate brown ponytail revealed and accentuated her bright turquoise eyes, which prevented anyone from noticing the crow's feet that settled as passing decades took their toll.

She, still giggling at her joke, threw herself next to her son on the bed and leaned over to Saul's shoulder. Despite having no clue why his mother was laughing or why she would be a vampire, Saul started laughing with her until tears began rolling down their cheeks, and he hugged his mother tightly.

'Have you not read any vampire novels, Saul? I thought I gave you a copy of Dracula,' Daisy giggled, still trying to control her laughter to explain the joke. 'A vampire, can't come inside someone's residence unless invited. If you knew it, I think you would have understood the joke. I think it was funny.'

'I think then I'll need to brush up my knowledge of vampire folklore. You never know when it will become handy. But at least then we settled that you're not a vampire,' Saul smiled back, still enjoying his mother's happiness.

'Let's not jump to conclusions.' She said and pointed to the mirror. 'I am living in this house, so I have implicit permission to go anywhere. To be on the safe side, you should check whether my reflection appears in a mirror.'

'I'll do that, Mom. Some other time,' Saul said. He then gave a kiss on his mother's forehead and filled his lungs with the vanilla scent that reverberated through his mind, resurrecting one broken fleeting memory entangled with childhood dreams after another: his mother dropping him to school for the first time, waking up to a kiss and a gift on a birthday morning, finding consolation in her bosom after a loss that he can't recall now but wrecked his small world then. Above all, one scene flash flooded before his eyes.

It was the first day of the third grade. Students were shepherded into their respective classrooms by their parents. His mother put Saul's bag and lunch in his locker and walked him to one of the front desks near the window. A couple of minutes before the classes were to start, Saul attempted to hug her goodbye. She grabbed him by his little shoulders and stopped him.

'Your friend, Emil, is looking at us. He lost both his parents last month. He must be lonely. Go to him, please,' she whispered and waved at Emil, sitting at the back of the classroom, looking at his peers, saying goodbye to their families. To this day, Saul cringed with shame and self-loathing as hatred momentarily filled him for Emil, as the orphan denied him a deserved embrace.

He took his mother's right hand in his palms and kissed the hands that gave him life. '*One day,*' Saul thought, '*I will kiss and hug her for the last time without knowing it. Such is the natural procession of life. I will remember her, and maybe my children will also remember her. Then, it will be as if she never existed. I can sit beside her for all my life, telling her how much I care about her and love her. But when the time comes to say farewell, all the time spent together will never be enough. Like the lovers trying to squeeze in one last kiss before the conductor blows the final whistle. One more and one more. Delaying the inevitable. How many kisses are enough not to miss someone? There is no hug tight enough to last for eternity. Does Sophie's mom miss hugging and kissing her already?*'

'What's bothering you, Saul? You look miserable since yesterday, and you didn't want to talk to me. Did you fight with Poppy?' she asked. '*Not yet,*' Saul thought to himself. '*Planning to do that tomorrow.*'

'School work. Graduation. College applications. You know,' Saul said all the things that did not really bother him while fidgeting with his fingers.

'Is Mrs. Pallas still creating trouble for you? I can come and talk to her tomorrow. They say you should not talk bad about their teachers in front of your kids, but you know I hate that toad,' she sniffed and kept glancing at the mirror, maybe trying to avoid meeting Saul's eyes or maybe just making sure that she was not an immortal beast.

'I'll handle her, don't worry,' Saul said, laughing. He remembered the first day of school after he intercepted Sophie's fate. A student plucked him out of mathematics class and told him to go to Mrs. Pallas's room, where he found out his parents were waiting for him. His dad's ears turned red with a mix of open embarrassment and veiled anger while his mother wore a mask of neutral expression, shadowing a tearful, muted pride. 'Take a seat, Saul. We need to discuss your reckless and irresponsible action with your parents. This is not how a responsible citizen acts. But I think we can amend your ways. I believe in you.' Mrs. Pallas said to Saul.

'Is she still forcing you to take the "Suicide Philosophy" class?'

'Yes. Don't worry. Only a couple of weeks left.'

'Did Mr. Lewis...' she hesitated for a bit, looking for the right words and masking the trembling of her voice, or at least trying to, 'put on a display?' Daisy's gaze shifted from the small Persian carpet they had acquired long ago on a family trip and back to her son.

'He did today. He showed how to cut your wrists.' Saul dismissed the question and waved his hand, jumping to his feet. 'Let's go to dinner.'

'Show me your arms, now!' she said and jumped to her feet as well. Saul had not seen her mother this angry before in a while, either. Her blue eyes turned into a wave of tsunami, ready to demolish what dared to stand in its way.

'I did nothing, Mom. Let's go. Dad will hear us.' Saul swore and displayed his arms, and turned them around.

'I am sorry, Saul,' Daisy said ever softly. The tide had quickly turned, and small waves trickled down her cheek, still mustering enough energy to demolish everything on its path in Saul's heart. 'Your sister took the same class,' she said and sat down on the bed again. 'When Chloe came back home that day, she showed me the fresh scars. "Look, Mommy, what we've learned. Isn't it cool? Now I know how not to cut my wrists depending on my mood." That was when your sister started getting obsessed and researched every way to kill yourself.' Then she walked to her son, grabbed his face in her palms, and vowed, partially to her son and partially to herself.

'I will not let that happen to you. I will talk to your dad tonight.'

'Please don't.'

***

Lamb shank stew, Saul's favorite meal, posed a first-degree burn threat to their tongues, so the three around the table were patiently waiting for the dinner to cool down to an edible temperature. It was obvious to Saul that Daisy had taken hours to cook the stew to cheer him up. It seemed unfair to Saul that something that took hours of labor to be prepared would only be enjoyed for a couple minutes and then forgotten. *Should there be an equivalency in the time spent for something and enjoyment derived from it?* Saul pondered while stirring his stew. *Hmm, then what about the statues and paintings in museums that have been enjoyed for centuries well past their master's entire lifespan? We do not want to tear them down for sure.'*

'City hall rejects the proposal to switch from coal gas to natural gas in the supply lines to homes citing financial concerns and lack of data on the latter's safety record,' the stoic news anchor from the TV kept filling the silence in the room.

Saul also felt guilt for his anticipation of trying the stew. He was still mourning for Sophie and feared what was going to happen when he confronted Poppy tomorrow. But he was hungry. *'Should a person who's mourning actively try not to enjoy anything even if it is unavoidable? Should I refuse to eat the stew and ask for some celery. Oh my god, who likes celery anyway? Would not a man notice a beautiful woman during a funeral?'* Saul thought some more and took a courageous sip from the stew.

'Annual crime rates hit a new low following the trend of decline that started decades earlier with the adoption of freed...' the TV anchor started another segment but was cut off by Daisy as she turned it off. Abraham, who was watching the news, glared at her but restrained his annoyance to a nasal, deep sigh, not out of his love for her but to shun an unnecessary conversation.

'I forgot to turn off the stew while chatting with Saul.' Daisy said and returned to the table. Abraham sufficed with a nod to recognize what his wife said and started eating his meal after his son managed to swallow a bite to lead the way. Abraham, balding in his late forties, was a well-built, athletic guy thanks to his frequent tennis matches and love for swimming. No one would guess that he was a bank executive, which was one of those jobs that was too comfortable to leave to follow one's dreams but not satisfying enough to wake up happy once in a while– a man of few words and even fewer emotions, no one caught him complaining anyway.

'How was your day, Saul?' Abraham recited a nightly dinner ritual he had learned from his father.

'It was okay. Nothing special, Father. How about you?' Saul repeated his part of the daily ritual.

'It's a busy time at work.' Abraham said to complete the dinner ceremony, and the family kept on eating. Then, they submerged back into a state of decaying loneliness that can only be achieved when one is surrounded by other people. Saul tried to remember when it was not a busy time at work for his dad. A big project was always followed by another busier and more important one.

'I will go talk to the counselor tomorrow morning. They're still forcing Saul to take Mr. Lewis's stupid class.' Daisy broke the silence halfway through her stew. She lifted her head and locked her turquoise eyes on Abraham. She didn't know whether she loved her husband now but remembered that she did once. The days he would hover around her. The moments he would blush when she put her hand on his knee. *That's what twenty years of marriage and the loss of a kid does to a love then,* she thought. She had become a rock on the shore getting washed over by waves, pitying the sea for throwing itself against her in anguish, never realizing her diminishing stature.

'No. You will not,' Abraham said without raising his head from the stew to meet his wife's eyes. He had once driven four hours across the country to look at them for half an hour.

'We can discuss it privately if you want, then,' Daisy conceded some ground but made it clear that she was not going to relent easily. She never liked arguing against her husband and followed her mother's advice to turn a blind eye and a deaf ear whenever the prospect of one arose. Sailing in uncharted waters of her character, she was trying her best to prevent the trembling of her hands. She lowered her head down to the stew.

'There is nothing else to be discussed. Saul is not a little kid. Do not interfere with his schoolwork,' Abraham said, seething, then put down his spoon on the glass table and finally raised his head, displaying his furrowed brow.

'I will not let what happened to Chloe happen to Saul, ' Daisy sniffed, losing the battle against her tears, put both of her hands on the table and stood up.

'I am sorry, Mom. Please don't get started. I'll handle it, don't worry. Let's talk later,' Saul interjected and walked over to his mom to make her sit down.

'What the hell happened to Chloe? She was an adult who made her own damn decision!' Abraham bellowed and slammed his right fist on the table, nearly flipping over his soup plate, sending bits around the table, then pointed his index finger to his wife. 'You wanted to condemn her to suffer for your own happiness.'

'That's not true!' Daisy shrieked back. Her face was contorted in a way that swung between anger and sadness, depending on the momentary position of her lower lip. 'I loved her. I still love her. I would give my life to bring her back,' Daisy claimed and pounded her chest like a male orangutan goading his opponent to a fight.

'Please, I'm sorry. Please, stop.' Saul said, and this time, tried dragging his mother out of the kitchen, to no avail. He only managed to pull her feet a couple steps away from the door while she squirmed like a giant tuna in his hands, trying to get back to the sea.

'You turned the house into a constant funeral with incessant mourning. Rather than wishing to die for her, maybe you should have tried living for us!' Abraham roared, stood up, and swung his arm over the table to throw everything on it to the floor. Saul saw veins in his dad's face that he had never seen before. 'And you, stop apologizing. Be a man. What are you saying sorry for?'

Saul bit his tongue not to say sorry for apologizing. His head started spinning, and his vision blurred; he felt disengaged from his own body to become a bystander to a three-way fight.

'I'm sorry that I'm not heartless as you are,' Daisy fired back.

'If so, then do not live with a heartless man anymore. You know what? We're done. I am not going to put up with you anymore.' Abraham stormed out of the kitchen door. When Saul tried to follow him. He told his son to stay with his mother.

When Saul returned to the kitchen, his mother was on her knees, crying her eyes out. Saul wished he knew what to say. He didn't, so he sufficed with kneeling down beside her.

***

Poppy still had not shown up minutes before the zoo tour was to start. Every Tuesday morning of their senior year, Poppy and Saul met with seventh graders in front of the gate of the zoo to show them different animals brought to the city from all corners of the world: colorful butterflies and poisonous frogs from the Amazon, big lazy cats from Africa and various boisterous primates from Asia to name a few. But today, Saul, dressed in khakis from tip-to-toe, supposedly like the true adventurers who collected all the specimens enclosed in the cages, stood alone in front of the fifty kids who were getting chattier by every second. Saul decided to wait a

couple more minutes for Poppy to start the tour. At the same time, he was oscillating in the back of his mind between anger and worry for Poppy; *'Am I going to
hug her tight and tell her I was worried sick or grab and shake her shoulders and ask
her how can you do this to us?'* Saul pondered and momentarily imagined Poppy
walking towards the Farewell Tree: an image that blinded him with fear, an occasion which both reactions Saul was contemplating would be considered apt by
many betrayed lovers.

'Where is your girlfriend?' The zoo's tour director asked Saul. He was a friendly
guy in his late fifties with a slight drinking problem and a wife who complained
all the time. It was hard to tell which came first, his drinking problem or his wife
starting to sleep with the neighbor. But at least the director was always nice enough
to schedule Poppy and Saul together.

'I don't know. She should have been here long ago.' Saul pretended to look at
his watch, but his brain did not register what time it was.

'Maybe she's sick. You'll have to do it alone today,' the director said and wiped
the sweat from his brows and balding scalp. 'Damn, today is really hot. The kids
have to go back to school before lunch.'

'Okay, sir'

Saul waved his hands above his head and asked the group to follow him
through the entrance. Usually, it was Poppy who made the introductory speech,
but Saul had to shoulder the responsibility today. 'Where are you?' Saul muttered
to himself.

***

'Why do we have zoos?' Saul asked the group while climbing backward over a small
hill, a skill he had honed over the last months, to the silvery plastic dome, which
was big enough to cover a small Olympic stadium.

'To see the animals have sex!' a tall ginger kid in front of the group jested, and
the rest of the kids erupted in laughter. On a normal day, Saul would have laughed
along with the kids and enjoyed chaperons blushing and scrambling towards the
boy to admonish him. But he was not in a good mood today.

'Now I know who the class clown is. You're on a school trip for learning. I am
not here to babysit and entertain you; don't waste my time. If you want to tell

jokes, save them for an open mic night,' Saul said to the ginger kid, and the commotion subdued immediately. 'Anyone else want to give an answer? A serious one this time.' Saul asked without a smile on his face and kept climbing the hill.

It was indeed boiling hot today, and he was glad of the red and green oak trees that sided the rest of the curved path to the dome to provide some intermittent shade. '*Is Poppy under a shade now? Her skin turns pink, and she gets easily sunburnt,*' Saul worried about his girlfriend. Then, his thoughts drifted to Sophie. '*Did Sophie used to get sunburnt easily also?*' None of the kids, as they were all shell-shocked from their tour guide's rant, dared to give an answer that would have dragged Saul from his imaginary worries about a dead girl's skin care. Then Saul felt sorry for admonishing the boy in front of his peers and teachers, so he gave him one more chance and pointed to the boy.

'Try one more time, buddy. Why do we have zoos?' Saul said with a crooked fake smile spanning ear to ear.

'Hmm. Maybe to save some extinct animals?' the boy guessed, blushing more to match his hair color with a look of determination to save face.

'Bravo!' Saul congratulated the boy and gave him two thumbs up. 'Zoos play a crucial role by doubling as a reservoir for critically endangered species that might experience a population collapse or even a total wipe-out. Simultaneously, they actively try to reintroduce animals born in captivity to boost dwindling wild populations.'

'But don't animals miss the wild until the zoo releases them?' asked a girl from the class, which started slowly relaxing and buzzing again.

'Well, for the ones that are born in captivity, they've never seen the wild before. So, they can't miss what they've never known. Can they?' Saul answered the question. Now they had arrived at the doors of the dome. 'But to be honest, most of the animals here are never going to be released to the wild. Zoos are also a great educational tool for the public to see what other beings we share the planet with. I just want you to keep in mind that the sole purpose of these animals is not for your entertainment.'

'Except for the baby goats.' Poppy said and appeared behind Saul while cradling a month-old baby goat. 'Their sole purpose is entertainment here.'

'Baah. Baah,' the spotted kid with floppy ears chimed in, looking comfortable, snuggled to Poppy's bosom.

Girls immediately swooned over the goat and let out cries of adoration. 'Can we please hold it too, please?'

'We're going to visit the petting section of the zoo after we finish our trip. There, all of you will get a chance,' Poppy promised the girls and handed over the baby goat to a nearby tour guide who was waiting to pick up the kid and return it to its nanny. 'Also, sorry that I was late. I went to pick up the kid to show what's waiting for you at the end of the trip.' Poppy winked at the group, walked past Saul, and swung open the doors of the dome. 'Of course, given that you behave well and participate.'

***

'Oh my god! It is so humid and hot in here,' the group cried out in chorus.

'Yes. It needs to be. The dome replicates the original natural habitat of the plants, animals, and insects that are here: The Amazonian Rainforests.' Poppy explained as she led the group over a glass footbridge replicating a small river bank, that went over the nest of freshwater caimans.

'Wow, look at the alligators,' a bespectacled inquisitive girl gushed over the reptiles, which could have been mistaken for ornamental statues if the minuscule movements in their nostrils and bellies had not revealed their true nature. Trying to get a better look, the girl leaned over the railings, almost losing her balance.

'Be careful. Don't lean over,' Saul warned the girl and pulled her back to her feet.

'They're not alligators, but caimans from the crocodilian family. You can call the difference from their snout shapes. Crocodiles have V-shaped snouts,' Poppy said and led them further towards the heart of the man-made jungle. The biologist curators of the dome had done a remarkable job of replicating a slab of the forest from the dense bushes surrounding the trees, which were almost piercing through the semi-translucent ceiling, to a curved low-current river coursing through. The dome was also bustling with life everywhere, from the gaily colored macaws and toucans sitting on low branches behind nets to occasional lizards scrambling away from noisy toads that were trying to catch flies buzzing by on the small river banks.

'What are those?' The bespectacled, inquisitive girl tugged on Saul's shoulder and pointed to giant green circular trays, big enough for a toddler to sleep on, floating on part of the river. 'Those are called *Victoria Amazonica,* giant water lilies. They are connected to the small purple flowers outside the green trays.' Saul pointed to the various lilies down below from another footbridge. At another footbridge in front of him and the bespectacled girl, Poppy gathered the class around a glass cage containing colorful frogs the size of a large coin. 'They are called dart frogs, and they are the most poisonous animal in the world,' Poppy informed the kids and stepped aside so they could get a better look. 'Who can tell me the difference between venomous and poisonous?'

'Venomous animals are the ones that can kill with a bite or a sting. Poisonous are the ones that you shouldn't eat,' the bespectacled girl yelled from Saul's side and ran to join her friends. 'Yes, true,' Poppy affirmed and high-fived the girl, now standing next to her. 'I'll let you hold a baby goat first.'

Saul was getting more agitated with each passing second, enraged by his girlfriend's nonchalance. He was resisting the urge to sprint to Poppy, grab her by the arm, drag her outside in front of the kids, and start yelling, *'Tell me everything you talked with Mrs. Pallas about. Did you just take me to the park to witness Sophie hanging herself? How could you deceive me? What did I do to you?'* He also had started to blame Poppy for the fight that happened yesterday at home. *'If you didn't drag me to the park, my mom wouldn't have been worried about me,'* Saul started fuming internally and hyped himself up.

***

They passed over another footbridge that led to a small square where palm-sized butterflies created a whirlwind of rainbows. 'If you stand still, they might land on you, but please do not try to grab them,' Poppy warned the kids and all of them became faithful statues of themselves. One of the kids let out occasional cries of joy when a disappointed butterfly briefly hovered over them to seek non-existent nectar. Then a butterfly landed briefly on Poppy's nose and seemingly made eye contact with her while slowly fluttering its wings to display the flashy cornflower blue center, contoured by a black band dotted with white and red dashes on the upper side and a brownish downside decorated with yellow-hued dartboards doubling as soulless eyes. With or without the butterfly, with or without the setting deceiving him, Saul admitted his love for Poppy. '*Two of the universe's beautiful creations looking at each other.*' He wanted Poppy to look him in the eye and lie, tell him she was not involved, take him for a fool, and say she never talked to Mrs. Pallas. His heart was in the ironic anguish of a man whose hand was burning with ice.

'It's a morpho butterfly,' Saul noted for the crowd and walked among the still figures towards Poppy. 'Its bright blue side is to attract mates, and its brown side is to deter potential predators.' When his girlfriend was at arm's distance, he shooed away the butterfly from Poppy's nose, 'It chooses which one of its faces to show depending on the circumstances.' He then leaned over to Poppy and whispered, 'Just like you.'

'You know cheesy pick-up lines never worked on me,' Poppy shot back, dismissed Saul's jab, and took a step away from him. 'Let's head for the exit. Our next stop is the primates,' she announced and showed the way to the class. The inquisitive bespectacled girl appeared next to Poppy this time, beaming with excitement. 'It was really cool! I wish I had a camera with me,' she gushed.

'Let me give you a secret. I rub a little drop of honey-maple syrup on my nose to attract butterflies. This is the first time it worked,' Poppy confided in the girl and sent her away. 'Go join your friends.'

'Why did you take me to the park, Poppy?' Saul glowered and grabbed his girlfriend just above her right elbow. 'I talked to Mrs. Pallas. Tell me.' Now they were alone at last, apart from the indecisive butterflies, hungrily searching for food and mates. On the corona of a purple passion flower behind Poppy, two morpho butterflies met for a dinner date.

'What are you talking about?' Poppy lied and tried to pull her arm away.

'Don't play dumb, Poppy,' Saul said, pulling her closer to him and smelling her honey-infused perfume once again. 'Please!' Saul said and squeezed her arm more.

'You're hurting me!' Poppy moaned and pushed Saul back with her free arm, or at least tried to.

'Then speak!' Saul said, unfazed but coming back to his senses a bit, letting go of her arm.

'We decided that it was the best for you. I did it for you.' Poppy groaned, still rubbing her arm.

'Who are 'we' that decided for me? You lied to me!' Saul said and pushed Poppy back with his finger. Then he saw one of the young chaperons looking at them with her mouth slightly ajar.

'The kids had a question about one of the insects in the cage,' a young chaperon apologized for being a witness and pointed behind her to the kids.

'Sorry for that, I'm coming.' Poppy said, blushing, and walked towards the kids.

***

Theo's eyes started to hurt from the light reflecting from the white walls. He had been waiting in the interrogation room for at least an hour. Because the police took his watch and there was no clock on the barren walls, he wasn't sure, but he must have waited for at least an hour. He studied what was there to study in the room: the wooden desk, two plastic chairs, and a windowless steel door. *Something is off in this room,* he thought to himself. Something in its layout. Finally, he decided that it was the dimensions: the room was a cube. All the other rooms he had been in before were rectangular. But at least the cube room had proper air conditioning. Not all rectangular rooms had it.

Following a metallic cling, the steel door opened, and the same sergeant who invited him for questioning appeared with a coffee cup in his hand. With his free hand, the sergeant pulled the plastic chair and placed it so close to Theo that their knees almost touched each other when the police officer sat down.

'Did you want one also?' the sergeant asked when he saw Theo eyeing the coffee cup on the table. The driver shook his head. He was just surprised that the sergeant put the coffee cup so close to him. A criminal could easily snatch it from the table and pour its hot content on the police officer to hurt him. But Theo was no criminal. 'A couple of eyewitnesses claim they saw the intern driving the train.'

'They must have been confused. She was just standing there helping me.'

'Okay. That's what I thought too,' the sergeant said, smiling, and took a small sip from the cup. 'In any case, we also asked the intern to come over for questioning so she could corroborate your statement. You see. Regular bureaucracy.'

'What's the point of this!' Theo asked and pulled his chair back from the sergeant, who instead laid back in his. 'Even if she was driving, it's legal,' he said and crossed his arms on his chest.

'Nobody said it wasn't,' the sergeant replied and took another sip from his coffee. 'However, providing a false statement about an investigation to a law enforcement officer *is*. Besides, you know very well that after the O-train is built, passenger trains are required to slow down near the stations even if they aren't planning to make a stop to deter the jumpers.'

'The guy was *not* a jumper!' Theo screamed and slammed his fist on the table, almost knocking off the coffee cup. 'He was pushed.'

'All the same,' the sergeant replied and smiled at Theo. 'Glad you didn't want coffee. You don't need any more caffeine.' Upon the sergeant's remarks, Theo took a deep breath and momentarily closed his eyes.

'What am I accused of? Why am I here? Over speeding?'

'Well, prosecutors decide which charges to bring. This was initially all about the murder. But I would say the prosecutor might decide to bring charges of gross negligence and endangering public safety against you.' With a big gulp, the sergeant finished his cup and crumbled it in his hands. 'Why don't you just tell me the truth?'

'I told you a hundred times,' Theo said, breathing in between every word. ' I was driving the train, and we were going slightly above the speed limit. That's all. Maybe right at the speed limit.'

'At the time of the crash, you were fifteen minutes ahead of schedule,' the sergeant said and pulled his chair closer to Theo again so that their knees once again almost touched each other. 'If you were going at the speed limit, how did that happen?'

'I don't know where you're coming up with those numbers,' Theo said and pushed his chair back once again, but it hit the wall. The sergeant didn't follow him any further, stood up from his chair, and walked towards the door.

'I got what I need. Do you have anything else you want to tell me?'

'Am I free to go?' Theo asked and threw his hands up in the air. He felt his face turning red as a flurry of worries started taking over him. What would he do if he lost his train driver's license? What was he going to tell his wife?

'Sure. Just don't leave the city. A couple of signatures and you can sit at home and wait for the court date,' the sergeant said and reached for the doorknob. 'Next door, we have the suspect.' He pointed to the wall with his head. 'Once we wrap up his interrogation, a court date can be set.'

***

The suspect's calmness and warm smile bothered the sergeant. He eyed the suspect and tried to determine whether it was the coolness of a man sure of the inevitable vindication or was it the apathy of a cold-blooded murderer? The sergeant pulled the chair close to the suspect, who in turn positioned his chair even closer so that their knees touched. The sergeant reflexively moved his chair back, which he regretted immediately. The suspect didn't react but kept the cool smile in place.

'Why did you kill him?'

'I told you, Officer. I didn't. He tripped. I was trying to catch him,' the suspect said, putting his left arm on the table and opening his palm. 'Why would I kill him?'

'I don't know. You have to tell me.'

'There's nothing to tell. It was an unfortunate accident.'

'There's a station full of people who saw you push the guy.'

'Think, sir,' the suspect said and leaned forward in his chair. 'How feasible do you think it is that the entire station was watching us before the unfortunate accident? I don't think anyone at all was watching us. They saw us when the guy tripped, and I failed to catch him,' the suspect said and leaned back. 'The human brain is amazing but also deceptive,' he said and tapped his head. 'It fills the missing parts to create a meaningful whole. But you can't construct a truth out of a thousand lies.'

'Was it a work problem?' the sergeant asked, but the suspect didn't answer this time and kept on smiling. 'Did he sleep with your wife?'

'I'm single,' the suspect replied. The sergeant noticed a slight twitch on the man's upper lip but couldn't be sure how to interpret it. He was indeed single on the records. '*Maybe a secret lover?*' he thought to himself.

'Just a run-of-the-mill psychopath then.' Upon seeing that he would get no further reply, the sergeant stood up and pushed his chair under the table. 'Well, I hope it was something worth spending the rest of your life in prison for.'

'I won't'

***

To cool off under the scorching sun, a silverback gorilla was munching on ice-covered fruits dangling from a rope. The kids were warned beforehand not to tap on the glass to try to goad the animal to perform its signature chest thump and scream. But given the state of the elder gorilla, the warning was needless. The silverback took a break from the dangling fruits, stood up, and locked his gaze on the small bushes in his enclosure. Maybe he heard something creeping among them or had a flashback to a time when he'd had a harem at his native home near the Congo River, a time when he indeed thumped his chest. A moment later, he sat back and kept munching on the dangling iced fruits, a delicacy he never had back at home but, if given the option, still would not have traded for his harem. In his dreams, he had both a harem and the iced dangling fruits. In his nightmares, he was in an enclosure with nothing but iced dangling fruits.

A community of busy chimpanzees occupied the next cage. On the ground, a couple of younglings mock-wrestled, each trying to dominate the other, while a couple of grandmothers, perched on a pole combing each other for fleas, threw disapproving looks down at them. Three old truck wheels were tied on the branches of an oak tree for the chimps to enjoy their retirement as makeshift swings. In the middle of the cage, there was an anthill and a group of primates poking the ant nest's openings with sticks and thin leaves they found around the bushes. In front of their cage, a middle-aged tourist guide imitated the apes' movements: poke the nest with the stick, wiggle the stick, pull the stick back, and eat the hapless ants still hanging on. The tourists wowed in unison and took a step closer to the window.

Poppy stood in front of the next enclosure down the line, which held rhesus macaques:

'Who can tell me the difference between apes and monkeys?' Poppy said and scanned the group, who stood in silence. 'The easiest way to tell them apart is that nearly all monkeys have tails, and no ape has a tail.' She answered her question and rolled her eyes at the ignorant indifference of the group.

'These are monkeys then,' a kid from the group aptly pointed out.

'Yes. And you also get to hold a baby goat!'

The macaques in the cage were hanging around in small groups; some of them chewed on leaves and fruits, while others tentatively groomed each other for any parasites. Alert for any potential threats to their babies, there were also a couple of new mothers, under a blissful shade, who were breastfeeding their newborns.

Saul leaned over the railings of the cage at the tail of the group, which huddled around Poppy. In his mind, he was playing over the argument they had again and again. Then, he imagined a scene when Mrs. Pallas and Poppy shook hands over the agreement. '*Was Sophie there also?*' Saul wondered. '*Did they kindly ask her to postpone her suicide so it would coincide with Poppy's birthday?*' He squeezed the hot metallic railings until his knuckles turned white, then spat into the moat separating the cage from the tourists. He took a deep breath that filled his lungs with the acrid scent of animal excretions, exacerbated by the heat, which revulsed him further.

'Rhesus macaques are highly intelligent creatures. That's why scientists around the world used them for many social and psychological experiments,' Poppy said and pointed to mother monkeys who were tending to their offspring. Saul looked over his shoulder at Poppy. Her face, which great Renaissance sculptors could have used as a model for a statue dedicated to a debauched Greek nymph, was unfazed by the confrontation. However, pulling down strands of her hair, as she always did when nervous, revealed the true nature of her soul's turmoil; Chestnut wavy hairs became taunt violin strings that plucked a couple of notes from a Paganini Caprice then rolled back to a curl before reaching the crescendo, dashing hopes of a quick pleasure. '*She knew what was going to happen and prepared for it.*' Saul thought. '*From the moment we walked into the park hand in hand. From the moment I felt her warm breath over my face, sitting on the bank. She knew it. Why did she betray me? I need to talk to her,*' Saul agitated himself further.

'A groundbreaking experiment was performed on them a while ago that provided us with great insight into understanding the role of nature vs nature in development. Who can tell me what nature vs nurture is?' Poppy queried and once again scanned the crowd. She shifted her weight from left to right, front to back, then pulled down the pleated khaki skirt slightly more down to her kneecaps. She was self-conscious about a birthmark just above her left knee and usually avoided wearing short skirts, but the sun today forced her to put her pride aside. The bespectacled girl put her hand up and raised on her tiptoes to answer the question. Poppy ignored her and asked, 'Anyone else who can tell me?' Seeing none of them knew or did not care enough to answer, she resorted back to the girl.

'Nature is what we have in our genes, and nurture is how the environment we are born in shapes us,' the girl recited the sentence she'd memorized from a biology book she read while preparing for the trip to the zoo.

Poppy sufficed with an affirmative nod and went on to explain the details of the experiment. 'Newborn babies were separated from their mothers and the rest of the clan a couple months after they were born,' Poppy said and licked her lips; she regretted not taking a lipstick with her. 'Then those babies stayed in complete isolation for up to a year.'

Some kids gasped in horror and covered their wide-open mouths with their hands. Some took another closer look at the macaque mothers in the cage, still cradling and breastfeeding their babies.

'Didn't those babies miss their mothers? Mothers must also have felt devastated!' The kids broke in and voiced their concerns for the well-being of monkeys that, unbeknownst to them, had already been euthanized years ago.

'Well...' Poppy shrugged. 'It was a necessary sacrifice to advance our scientific understanding. Scientists did not do those experiments for fun.' She tried to justify the moral side of the tests and took a step back from the crowd to let the kids get a better view of the monkeys.

'You are quick to ask for other's sacrifices.' Saul put on a smile, appearing next to Poppy, and put his elbow on her shoulder. 'Those experiments were unethical and now are banned.' Saul assured the kids.

'Do not interrupt me again. Please!' Poppy hissed and threw off Saul's arm.

Saul took a step away from Poppy to let her finish the explanation.

'Then those baby monkeys, isolated nearly for their entire life, had their own kids in return,' Poppy began to continue her story once again. 'You see, those babies had never seen how other monkeys raised their babies as they were brought up by researchers,' Poppy said and pointed to a monkey mother who shifted her baby from one breast to the other. 'The question was whether the legendary motherly instincts were going to kick in and those isolated monkeys were going to be turned into perfect mothers,' Poppy went on and pretended to cradle a baby herself. 'But that wasn't the case,' Poppy said and opened her arms to drop the imaginary baby. 'Most of those mothers completely ignored their babies after birth and left them to starve. Some chewed the baby's feet, and a few crashed its skull as the crying disturbed them,' Poppy said and pretended to stomp something on the ground and twisted her ankle as if she was putting out a discarded cigarette butt. 'In a single generation,' Poppy hit a crescendo as she reached the end of the story, 'In any society, it is possible to wipe out what evolution built in thousands of years.' She finished and licked her lips once again and cursed under her breath for not bringing a lipstick. 'Now, before we move on to the big cats, who wants some ice cream?'

***

After the last kid had bought her ice cream, pistachio dipped in chocolate sauce from the truck, the group walked on to see the big cats, the final destination before the petting zoo. Saul skipped on ice cream and answered questions from a couple of boys, who recently had started to discover their own sexuality, about the mating habits of monkeys: Do they avoid having sex with their siblings and parents? Are they polyamorous? Can female monkeys tell who the real father is? 'Yes. Yes. I don't know.'

Then he walked towards the front of the group to talk to Poppy again, who was massaging her lips with ice cream. She had already been sunburned, even before noon, and minor blemishes appeared around her mouth and nostrils. Her khaki t-shirt, whose underarms showed extended dark spots, was too tight, so she kept on tugging its hem with her free hand to find momentary comfort. Saul felt he was approaching a stranger. He thought about Poppy's theatrics in explaining the experiment, which he had seen scores of times. Pretend to cradle a monkey baby, drop it on the ground, crash its skull, and ask the kids if they want ice cream. That was what the director taught them during the training: 'It helps get our message across easier.' Whatever *that* was. He also did the show a couple of times himself. He never put much thought into it. There was no real baby that was hurt.

He was not the one who designed the experiment, and none of the kids were going to remember it, anyway. *'But somewhere in a lab, there was a real baby monkey which was neglected by its mother. Did the baby realize something was wrong, or did it just assume that's how the world works? Maybe the mother thought her years of isolation was the norm and what eventually waited for her baby, so, out of compassion, she spared her offspring from the horror.'* Saul thought. Poppy's face flashed across his mind once again, lit up with excitement to share what she had memorized, darkened with aloofness from the banality of repetition. *'Does a murderer feel the same guilt for the first stab as the tenth stab?'* Saul wondered and imagined stabbing someone, lying face down. His hands and face covered in blood, Saul turned over the body to find himself looking into a ghost peering back from a red-hued mirror. He shook off the daytime nightmare and approached Poppy:

'I want to talk to you.' Saul said, slowing down to match Poppy's gait.

'Not now,' she shrugged, massaged her lips with ice cream, and took a bite from the cone.

'You've been avoiding me since Monday. Just tell me what happened. I want to believe you. Please,' Saul insisted on an explanation as they passed by a puma cage.

'I never understood why you...' Poppy started but hesitated for a moment to choose the right word, '...stopped her on the day of the picnic.' She took another bite from the ice cream and turned to face Saul.

Now, the kids were huddled around the railings of the enclosure, looking down at the graceful honey-colored puma strolling in the cage. The puma then tilted his face up and focused his azure gaze on the crowd looking down upon him and licked his upper lip.

'I... I...' Saul started concocting an answer, but he now stuttered to decide how to describe his action, 'I had saved her from dying,' he said. Mrs. Pallas's face and rings flashed before his eyes. 'I saved her,' he repeated to himself, Poppy, Mrs. Pallas, and Sophie's specter. He felt as if he was explaining why one plus one equals two and getting frustrated at her insistence to deny it. But as the word 'saved' echoed inside his ears, other numbers and decimals started flooding his mind, along with a gaping doubt.

'Well, how did that turn out?' Poppy asked, marching on to the next enclosure, massaging her lips with the remaining bits of the ice cream at the bottom of the chewed-off cone.

'What the hell does that mean?' Saul said, raising his voice gradually with each syllable. 'Poppy. Poppy. Poppy, I am talking to you,' he said and followed her to the next cage.

'Now here we see the great...' Poppy turned around to the kids.

'You lied to me! Why did you want to go to the park?' Saul interrupted Poppy, grabbing her shoulder and turning her around. 'Why did you not tell me directly, let's go see Sophie, if it was normal, if it was the right thing to do? Did Mrs. Pallas force you?' Saul thundered, his face now turned purple with passion, uncharted new veins popped up in his brow, and he shook both of his fists at Poppy, who took a step forward towards him.

'Would you have come if I asked you?'

'Why would I ever?'

'To see her get relief from her pain. I thought you cared about her,' Poppy interjected, grinned, and took another bite from the cone. The kids were now standing in awe, witnessing the most interesting exhibit of the day. They had learned the most poisonous animal in the world was the dart frog; now they were learning that the most venomous bite comes from the tongue of a disillusioned lover right before the strong bond holding two souls together disintegrates.

Saul hit the cone out of Poppy's hand, pushed her back, and screamed, 'What do you want from me?'

'I was trying to help you, idiot!' Poppy said, stamped on the cone, and sent the remaining bits flying. 'If I didn't help you, Mrs. Pallas was not going to sign your application. Forget about that. You had to learn not to interfere in other people's lives. I was saving you,' she said and poked Saul's heart.

'So, you decided she had to die then!' Saul said and hit Poppy's hand away.

'Ha! Don't worry. It's your thing to decide who lives or dies. Isn't it?' Poppy asked. 'Sophie was okay with it. It was her idea. She thought it would bring closure to you also,' she said and pushed Saul's shoulders, almost causing him to tumble back.

'Liar! I hate you. You're a murderer!' Saul lifted his hand up to slap Poppy.

'Do it! Fu…'

'Enough with this!' the tour director appeared, alerted by the other staff to intervene.

'Help! She fell down inside. Help!' The kids began screaming.

Saul rushed towards them, now leaning over the railings of the enclosure. He looked down, and inside the moat circling the cage, the bespectacled girl was lying unconscious in the waist-deep water.

'She's drowning! Please do something!' one of the crying chaperons tugged on Saul's arm. In that instant, he felt he ceased to be a powerless bystander. Seeing no one else rushing to save the day, Saul jumped over the railing and slid down the slanted wall of the enclosure into the moat. On the way down, he tried to slow himself by using his hands and elbows against the rough surface, ending up bloodying both. As soon as he hit the bottom of the moat, luckily covered by overgrown moss that cushioned the impact, which strained his knees greatly, he sprang back to his feet. He lifted the girl's head out of the water and hit her back repeatedly.

'Come on, baby. Come on. There's no blood. It can't be that bad. Come on.'

Finally, the girl coughed up a bit of water, opened her eyes, and started crying again.

'My head hurts,' the girl whimpered and hugged Saul.

'That's okay, baby. You're fine. Let's get you out of here. What's your name, darling?' he ran his finger through the black satin hair, partly to calm her down and partly to check for any bumps.

'Alice,' the girl mumbled and groaned, 'I think I broke my left ankle.'

Saul checked her ankle without knowing what he was looking for. 'Probably, you've just twisted it a bit. Can you stand on it? Will you try it for me?'

The girl stood up, wobbling, and shifted her weight to the injured leg. 'It hurts, but I can,' she moaned and held on to Saul's arm. They then started shambling towards the end of the moat, where Saul hoped to climb out using the ladder. As the initial adrenaline waned, he started wondering, '*What's occupying this cage?*'

The crowd, looking down at them, let out a series of roars and pointed to something behind the moat's walls that Saul couldn't see. He pulled himself up the wall to peek at what was worrying the crowd.

'Can you hold on to the wall yourself for a minute, Alice?'

'What are they pointing to, Saul?' she asked and leaned against the wall. She leaned over to massage her ankle, then wiped away her incessant tears.

'I'll check now. Don't worry,' Saul told her and pulled himself up a bit. On his first try, Saul's fingers couldn't grasp the edge, so he fell back to the moat and hit his hip on the wall. On the second try, he pulled himself up a bit and managed to peek at what was sneaking toward them. Ten steps away, his eyes met two amber quartz eyes buried in a flurry of orange, black, and white flames. The creature, not used to guests in her cage, was startled and sprinted back to the opposite side of the enclosure and perched upon the slabs of stone. Saul cursed under his breath, let go of the edge, and slid back to the water again.

'What was it?'

'A tiger.'

***

'It won't be long before the tiger shakes off its initial surprise,' Saul thought as they walked towards the ladder. *'If she decides to jump into this narrow moat with us, we're screwed.'* He closed his eyes and concentrated on the brief image he saw behind the orange flames. 'The door of the cage is next to the stone slabs. We need to get there.' He then looked over at Alice, who was dragging her foot and wiping away tears with the back of her shaking hands.

'It'll be okay. Tigers aren't that aggressive. We're going to get out fine.' Saul lied to Alice and himself to calm them both down.

Saul kept on dragging Alice to the ladder. He lifted his head and looked at the crowd watching them. Blurry faces contorted with worry, indifference, and excitement. Vague noises originating from shapeless agape mouths lost their meaning once they reached Saul's ear drums. He wasn't looking for her specifically, but Saul couldn't help but notice that Poppy wasn't there. Last week, he would have sworn that she would be by his side until the bitter end. But he realized he did not know her. She was a beautiful shell created from his dreams, desires, and fears. '*I was probably the same for her*,' Saul conceded silently.

'I can't climb,' Alice said, pulling Saul out of his midday walking slumber.

'I'll go first and pull you up,' Saul said and held on to the warm steel railing of the ladder. His heart started fluttering in his rib cage. '*What if the tiger's waiting there and immediately pounces on me? Where are the cursed zookeepers? They should just shoot the tiger*,' Saul thought and lingered to delay facing the reality. He put his right foot on the first step and pulled himself up enough to see the enclosure. The animal, its head lowered and front shoulders moving up and down in their sockets, was again approaching, without rushing, to the moat where it had last seen the pair–a distance it could have covered before Saul would have been able to shout his undying love to Poppy mere days ago.

Saul looked at the door next to the stone slabs. While he was thinking that the door was probably locked and they would be mauled even if they reached it, two zookeepers appeared behind the bars, unfortunately, without carrying any rifles. They signaled Saul to climb out and slowly come towards them. Using little of his upper body strength but all his willpower, Saul climbed the ladder and finally put his knees on the ground. For a couple of seconds, he didn't raise his head from the earth beneath his palms. Grass blades were protruding between his fingers, as if Saul was petting the overgrown fur of a green beast without any pulse, yet so full of life. Yet so empty with death.

Scooping the bottom of his heart for whatever was left of his courage, Saul lifted his head. The tiger was wandering around a couple of trees at the other end of the enclosure. The animal seemed to have lost interest in the guests in the cage. Saul lowered his head once more, still crawling, turned back to the ladder and helped Alice climb up.

The zookeepers pointed them to walk to the door in an arc, following the edge of the moat to the walls and to safety. Standing on their shaking legs, they started their arduous pilgrimage. Saul felt the trembling of the little girl in his arms but felt lost for words to alleviate her fear. He opened his mouth to lie, 'There is nothing to fear,' but closed it back in truth.

Stretching its majestic muscular front legs, the tiger lowered her head, raised a giant hip, and made a question mark with her striped tail. Her gaze once again focused on the unexpected visitors. Following the opposite arc through the edge of the moat, the beast started approaching them.

'Don't look into its eyes! Keep backing away slowly!' shouted the zookeepers behind the safety of the bars.

The tiger, rightly assuming the instructions were not for her, kept approaching the duo along the arc of the moat. Right shoulder down, left shoulder up. Left paw front, right paw back.

When Saul took another look at the door, he saw that now two more zookeepers had appeared, one carrying a net gun and the other a rifle. Saul let out a sigh of relief. Help was here.

Saul kept following the arch after the moat ended. His fingers touched the wall behind their back, and he felt the rough surface comforting him. 'You're almost there. You rescued the girl. You'll live.'

30 more steps, and they would be behind the safety of the bars.

25 more steps.

20 more steps

Baring her ivory teeth, the tiger lowered her head and coiled down on her legs. She knew she could cover the distance between them in a couple of seconds. It was time to catch the prey.

'Run!' the zookeepers shouted. 'She'll attack! Run!'

The tiger started her sprint towards them. A couple more steps and she was going to be close enough to pounce.

Saul pulled Alice's arm and dragged her to the gate. Now there were 15 steps left. Defying the instructions, he lifted his head and looked into the tiger's eyes. He knew they wouldn't make it.

The zookeepers finally opened the gate, and the one with the rifle took aim at the tiger. But missed the shot.

Saul pushed Alice towards the door and sprinted back to the moat. Alice stumbled and fell flat on the ground. Seeing that her prey had miraculously split into two, the tiger hesitated for a moment to decide which one to chase. The split second gave the marksman another opportunity. Now, the bullet sank into the fur, slowly painting the tiger's torso into a calm sunset scene.

But it was not enough to take down the beast. She ran towards Alice, lying on the ground. For fear of shooting the girl, this time, it was the marksman's turn to hesitate. The tiger put her giant paw on Alice's head and shifted her weight on the girl, searching for the other prey. As the adrenaline subsided for the animal, too, the pain in her abdomen became more acute. The bullet had torn her intestines open.

Enthralled by the magic of witnessing a real tiger in action, Saul stood frozen on the edge of the moat. The tiger lowered her head to lick Alice's head under her paw. The marksman positioned himself again and pulled the trigger. Another bullet went to the tiger's hip. Still, it wasn't enough to take down the beast.

The tiger roared and pushed down on Alice's skull even harder, almost cracking it. Alice let out a shriek as the claws pierced the left side of her face, deep parallel marks to be carried for the rest of her brief life.

Saul shouted at the top of his lungs, burning his throat, 'Come here!' he yelled, flailing his arms, jumping up and down. 'Come to me!'

The tiger turned around and accepted the invitation at once. Covering the distance of a hundred human steps in the blink of an eye, the beast pounced on her next prey.

Saul took a step back and felt with his left heel that he was on the edge of the moat. The roaring orange thunder took off, and Saul saw the bottom of the face-sized paws up in the air. He ducked and rolled to the left but could not escape the hit from the left paw that dislocated his right shoulder. Blinded by the pain, Saul still stood up quickly but fell to his knees again. Then he heard a big splash. The tiger skidded and fell into the moat.

'Run!' the zookeepers yelled, waving their hands. Semi-blind, Saul took off at once to the door. He saw that one guard had already dragged the unconscious Alice behind the bars.

After 50 steps, he was going to be in as well.

He heard the roar, water splash, and the thud of paws on the ground.

Right shoulder down, left shoulder up. Left paw front, right paw back.

'Faster, boy, faster!'

But he was not fast enough.

Just 10 steps to the gate, a zookeeper slammed the door in his face. Saul saw the horror mixed with the agony on the guy's face. He forgave the zookeeper. He knew he couldn't make it there in time, anyway. He took another step to nowhere and stumbled. A flurry of orange fur flew over him and slammed into the wall next to the door. A drop of warm blood hit his face. He tried to stand up again, but the beast recoiled faster and was on top of him already. The tiger put her right paw on Saul's chest and leaned over, almost crashing his ribcage. Saul couldn't help but admire the majestic animal covered in blood. She was beautiful. If his rib cage was not getting crushed, he might have attempted to run his fingers through the striped fur. His mind started drifting. '*Would each color have a different texture? Probably not. Is it soft? Probably not either.*'

He tried to take a deep breath and filled his lungs with the pungent, musky smell mixed with blood and moss emanating from the animal. There was a sublime scent of buttered popcorn as well. A zookeeper once told him that a tiger's pee smells like buttered popcorn. 'I must be lying in her pee then,' he said. He thought of Poppy's honey-infused perfume, her wavy chestnut hair, her soft, milky skin, her betrayal, and her contagious laugh. 'I do not want to die. Please'

He heard the rifle being reloaded and cocked. The door of the cage flung open once more and hit the wall.

The beast, ignoring the zookeepers, bared her fangs and licked her prey's face. Saul screamed with pain and wriggled under the animal as the rough tongue filed down the side of his left cheek; a thousand needles were tearing through the skin. To stop the pain, one way or another, Saul threw a feeble left punch at the tiger's jaw. Just below the elbow, the animal caught Saul's arm mid-air in her mouth.

Saul went blind once again. The last things he saw were amber quartz jewels looking down on him and white whiskers covered in his own blood.

He could hear for a couple more seconds after darkness soothed him.

Cracking of a bone.

Screams.

A bang.

Sophie playing the guitar.

Part 4

He woke up to an electric shock through his left arm. At least, that's what Saul interpreted it as. Maybe an entire colony of ants was running inside his capillary veins and gnawing his fingers and his knuckles from inside. Another probability.

After a struggle, he opened his eyes. He was in a hospital bed. He tried to lift his head to see whether anyone else was inside the room but ended up only managing to open his eyelids slightly more. He was not sure whether he still had any vocal cords left, so he did not try to make a sound at all. With great effort, he rolled his head to the left and looked out the window depicting a twilight sky. '*Is it dusk or dawn?*' he thought to himself. '*I'm alive.*' He started crying again, partly with relief of existence, partly for the pain caused by the ants, and partly for Poppy. He then cried a bit for Sophie. He had not cried for his sister for a long time, either, so he cried a bit for her, too. As the tears started rolling down, they tickled the side of his nostrils, and his tongue tasted the salt. He tried to get his hand out of the blanket to wipe away the tears, but the weight of the blanket bested him.

'You're finally awake,' a nurse entered his room. 'Do you want anything, honey?' she asked and ran her fingers through his hair. The sensation of her nails grazing his scalp soothed him and scratched an itch that hadn't existed before she came in.

Saul turned his head away from the darkening twilight to see the nurse. She had a warm smile rooted in something humane, something sympathetic, deep in her heart. With her thumb, she wiped away Saul's tears and made him drink water from a straw.

'We administered some strong painkillers. They will wear off. Don't worry, honey.'

'My mom?' Saul muttered as water running through his throat once again blessed him with speech, even partially.

'Your parents are in the cafeteria. I'll go get them,' the nurse assured him and gave him some more water. 'Do you feel pain?'

'My left arm.' Saul said and took another sip from the water. 'It does hurt.'

'Okay. I'll give you some light painkillers then,' she said and walked back to the cart by the door. She had an elegant rhythm to her gait, an exotic mystery. The nurse leaned down to the last drawer and pulled out a syringe and a pink bottle with clear liquid inside. The clear liquid whirled inside the syringe as the nurse emptied the pink bottle. She then walked towards Saul, lifted the side of the blanket, and administered the drug through the cannula in his hand.

'Alice?' Saul asked and moaned as the drug caused an irritating pressure in his hand. 'The girl that was with me. You know?'

Once the syringe was empty, the nurse pulled back the needle and threw it in the bin next to Saul's bed. 'I know her. She was euthanized…' nurse looked at her watch, 'two hours ago.'

'Why?' Saul choked. 'I don't understand'

The nurse walked back to the cart and pushed it out of the door. 'Well, she definitely couldn't have lived with those awful claw marks on her face,' she said and started closing the door. She took another look inside the room and put her hands on the switch to turn off the lights. 'Also, she felt guilty for what happened to you and the tiger.'

'What?' Saul murmured as the drugs once again drew him to sleep. 'What happened to me?' he asked as curtains started rolling down before his eyes.

'I'll bring your parents and the doctors, honey,' the nurse said and turned off the lights.

This time, Saul cried a bit for Alice and the tiger just before he drifted away to another nightmare.

***

'Saul. My baby…' Daisy touched her son's cheek. 'It was just a bad dream. Wake up.'

Saul opened his eyes to two turquoise emeralds filled with tears. '*I put her through so much pain and anxiety*,' Saul thought.

'I'm sorry. I couldn't save the girl. I couldn't save Sophie. I couldn't save...' Saul sobbed.

'It's okay, baby.' Daisy stopped her son and wiped away her tears and Saul's. Tears from mom and son mixed in Daisy's finger. 'You're a hero. You're my hero.'

'I couldn't...' Saul started again.

'I read a story in a book a long time ago.' Daisy put her finger on her son's lips. 'Once upon a time, a king decided to burn a righteous man alive, for he refused to follow their way,' Daisy began and sat down on a chair next to Saul's bed and held his hand. 'By the way, do you want me to turn off the lights?'

'No. I want to see you, Mom.'

'I'm always here with you.' Daisy touched Saul's heart. 'Whether or not you see me.' she said and rose from her chair and kissed Saul's cheek. 'Where was I?'

'They were going to burn the man.'

'Yes. They set giant fires over the town square and tied the man to a catapult.'

'To throw him in the fire? A bit overboard.' Saul said and let out a sniff, a sliver of a laugh reminiscent of a happy day.

'Maybe.' Daisy smiled. She was a magnifying glass, amplifying the good in life. Or bad. But true nature never changes. 'Then a swallow flies over the town and lets out a drop of water from her beak on the huge fires blazing below. She rushes back over to a nearby pond to get some more water,' Daisy continued and pulled her chair closer so she could rest her elbow on Saul's bed while holding his hand. 'A couple of big birds, who were laughing at the futile efforts of the swallow, flew near her. "You can't put out the fire," the crow croaked, and the crane chortled. "I might not," the swallow tweeted back, "but I can show whose side I'm on."'

There was a knock on the door, and a doctor walked in with Saul's father, followed by the nurse who had visited him earlier.

'Hello. Please sit,' the young doctor, who looked like a film artist Saul could not remember from a movie with a happy ending, one of those where they get to live happily ever after, greeted the mother and son and gestured to Daisy to keep herself on the chair. 'Is there any bleeding? Do the stitches hold up?' she asked and walked to the other side of the bed. '*She walks like a newborn fawn,*' Saul thought. Daisy looked at the doctor and turned her head to the man whose wife she used to be. The young doctor put her hand on the blanket. Her eyes met Saul's eyes. '*She also has the eyes of a fawn,*' Saul thought. The eyes that ask to be taken to their mother. 'Are you lost? Are you looking for your mother? Quick, flee before the hunters come.'

'Did you tell him?' Abraham asked Daisy, crossing his arms on his chest as he leaned on the hinges of the door.

'He just woke up,' Daisy said and turned to Abraham and the doctor with pleading eyes.

'Tell me already!' Saul said as his system began shaking off the painkillers.

The doctor, in a swift move, lifted the blanket and threw it back over Saul to show what was not there. 'The tiger tore your arm. We had to amputate it below the elbow and sew up what was left.' She leaned over and lifted the stump a bit, covered in layers of gauze. 'There seems to be no bleeding.'

Saul's eyes went over where his arm used to be. The fingers he could not see were itching; the forearm that wasn't there was being crushed by a subdued version of the pain of the tiger's bite. As if his arm wasn't amputated but just invisible to the naked eye. 'I can still feel the pain,' Saul moaned and contorted his face. But closing his eyelids achieved little to ease the pain. Or frustration.

'Stitches can hurt.' The doctor nodded.

'Not the stitches,' Saul said without taking his eyes from the space where his arm used to be. 'I can feel my forearm and my fingers hurting.'

'We gave you some powerful painkillers,' the doctor said and walked back to the nurse, who handed her a bright pink agenda. 'They must be playing tricks on your mind.'

Saul wanted to argue with her and explain how he could almost twist his arm, make a fist, and snap his fingers. Now, he did mind that he could not do those, but he couldn't comprehend how he was still hurting. '*How can you alleviate pain in a limb that doesn't exist anymore?*' Saul wondered. It was as if someone had stabbed his mother in front of his eyes, and his guts were torn open. A severed connection that does not bring anything apart from pain now.

'Did you plan something specific?' the young doctor asked and flipped through the pages. She then stopped, and her finger slid down the page.

'What for?' Saul asked. He felt his mother squeezing his hand harder and turned his head to her. He had no doubt that the tiger bit his arm but tore off his mother's, too. A far greater sorrow and helplessness lingered in her eyes. She lamented that there were cruel problems that one could not solve even by the ultimate sacrifice of a mother. How worthless a mother's life can be that it fails to restore a mere limb. A life that created life cannot fold on itself either to restore or amend what is lost. A life so willing, a life so expendable, a life so full, a life yet not enough. Saul wished he could melt into thin air and become non-existent to not cause so much pain to her. This was the price of love. A sin you cannot atone for.

'If you want euthanasia, we need to schedule it,' the doctor replied, frustration mixed with amusement from iterating the obvious. She slid her finger down the page and flipped to the next one. 'Because it is midnight, our team is having a break. The next slot is at' she squinted her eyes on the agenda, 'at 10 AM tomorrow. Does it suit you? If it's too late, we can quickly arrange a rope. Normally, we'd have a gun, but it's late at night. It wouldn't be kind to wake up others. Or...'

'Shut up!' screamed Daisy and jumped up from her chair. Her face turned bright red in an instant. Her turquoise eyes were a testament that ice can indeed burn. 'Get out of the room at once! He doesn't want anything!'

'You're going to wake up people. Behave yourself!' hissed Abraham and peeled himself off from the door frame. 'Stop deciding for him,' he said and took a step towards Saul's bed. His lips twisted between contempt and pity. 'He can't possibly live like this. A half-man,' he said and thumped his chest. 'He's my son also. I love him, too. But I can neither turn back the clock nor save him now.'

'Shut up!' Daisy took a step towards Abraham and towered before him. A mother bear who was protecting her cub. 'You're not even anyone to us. You are nothing to us.'

'You can't condemn him to *this,*' he said and waved his arm at Saul. Now, his face also turned red.

'Enough!' Saul shouted, 'Enough,' he then whispered.

The doctor, her finger still on the agenda, and the nurse, her arms crossed on her chest and both sets of eyes wide open, witnessed the final scene from a marriage. They were like a family dog who had peed on the carpet in the living room; they had no idea why everyone was angry and why this had anything to do with them.

'I'll go home, Doctor. Will you discharge me tomorrow?' Saul asked. He did not try to hide the tears or the cracking of his voice.

'Sure. I'll arrange that,' the doctor said and left the room at once, along with the nurse. 'People these days,' she muttered to the nurse and shook her head.

'You're crazy. You poisoned him!' Abraham said, tapping on Daisy's chest, his eyes wide.

'Leave us alone, Father,' Saul asked his father and buried his head in the pillow. A new set of ants picked up the next shift and started gnawing at his ghost arm.

Like a fish plucked out of water, Abraham opened and closed his mouth a couple times. But eventually, he decided there was nothing for him there, so he jumped back to the sea and slammed the door behind his back.

Daisy walked to the door and turned off the lights. She didn't want Saul to see her crying again. She sat down next to the bed and held his hand again.

'What happened to the righteous man, Mom?'

'Does it matter, baby?'

***

Buttons had become his arch-nemesis. Before the amputation, he had never cared about his clothing, but it was a statement about him now. It was nearly three weeks after the incident, and he had already torn two shirts as they fell victim to his rage for their lack of cooperation in getting themselves buttoned easily. Daisy had bought sweatpants and buttonless t-shirts, but they were a no-go. Wearing them would be capitulating to buttons, and Saul was not a quitter. Buttons were a major struggle, but not the only one. Putting on socks was hard, and tying his shoes was maddening. It was mostly those little daily things that annoyed him. But what kept him awake at night were the endless hypotheticals. He never wanted to climb a mountain, but now, the prospect of not being able to reach a peak in his lifetime was impossible to accept. What if he wanted to become a juggler one day?

He carefully looked into his eyes in the mirror. He tried to etch the lines, veins leading into the dark hole of his pupils to his mind. The longer he looked at the reflection, the more estranged he felt from himself. He wasn't sure whether he would have recognized himself if the two of them crossed by each other in a narrow alleyway.

'Hello. Do I know you from somewhere?'

'Highly unlikely. I've never seen you before.'

He peeled his eyes from the mirror and looked down at his non-existent hand. There, he saw Alice wriggling under the tiger, claws piercing her face. At first, he was furious with the girl as his efforts were for naught. He had lost his arm so that she could live a couple more hours. Then, he thought maybe Alice was scared as well. Doctors and her family towering before her bed. Her mom, looking at Alice's face: 'She can't possibly go outside with that ugly scar.' Maybe Alice didn't even mind the scar at all, but screams of qualms of conscience drowned over her for his fate. He imagined leaning over to her and putting the girl's little face inside his only hand and caressing her scar. 'It's okay. We'll get through this.'

Above all, he could not forgive himself. 'I shouldn't have been arguing with Poppy. I should have been watching over the kids,' he muttered in his sleep every night and kept tossing in his bed. Sophie was also a constant staple in his dreams. In every scene, she was sitting somewhere strumming her guitar. Saul tried multiple times walking over to her, but a force was repelling him away. 'Tell me, Sophie,' he tried to shout, 'What is wrong? Maybe I can help?' but every time, his voice became muffled, and a force dragged him away. Sophie raised her head, put the guitar on the ground, and walked away. He was not getting much sleep at night.

Another shock of electricity went through the space where his arm used to be. Then, a pressure as if it was caught in an ever-tightening vice.

One thing that alleviated the pressure was putting a sock over the stump. Feeling the end of his stump somehow reminded his brain of the obvious that his arm was not there. Ergo, the pain should not be either.

'May I come in, baby?' Daisy knocked on the door and came in without waiting for the answer. 'Why are you packing your duffel bag?'

'Today is Friday. It's training day. You know we have our regional final in two weeks,' he said and leaned over to peek under his bed. 'Have you seen my shin guards?'

Daisy's face contorted with pain. 'You know...' she started but then stopped to look for the right words and twisted her hands. 'You know you just had the surgery. Your stitches were removed three days ago.'

'What you are saying, Mom?' Saul rose from under the bed with shin guards in his hand. 'I shouldn't play? I'm the captain of the team. I can't miss it. The team needs me,' he said, tucking his gear in the duffel bag and swinging it over his shoulder.

'No. Just be careful,' Daisy said and stepped aside from the door. She gave a small kiss as Saul passed by her.

***

He met Ezra, also with his own duffel bag, at the entrance of the school. Ezra stopped by Saul's home every day to drop off school notes and keep him company as he recovered. Now, on the first day of school after the accident, Ezra was again standing beside him.

As they entered the corridors of the school, Saul's expectation was that everyone would gawk at him and whisper to one another. To a certain extent, he would have understood, even forgiven, their demeanor, as he was likely the first disabled person they had seen in their lives. At least one who was not walking or crawling to a scaffold, a gun, or a drug bottle. But now, everyone was *not* looking at him. He had hyped himself up to slam the first student he could reach to the lockers and scream, 'What are you looking at?' Now he was thinking of doing the same but asking, 'What are you *not* looking at?'

Eventually, Saul realized that those students only existed as long as he paid attention to them. So, he decided to kill all the students around him going on to their classes. He'd only let Ezra exist.

'Do you remember Sophie?'

'I do.'

'I was thinking about her.'

Saul turned to the side to see his friend, who fell into silence. Ezra was not looking at him either, but that didn't bother him. 'Did she have any friends? You were partners in the physics lab, right?'

'I don't know much,' Ezra thawed after much consideration. He then looked back at Saul and realized his friend was not going to stop questioning him. 'She once mentioned that she was dating a guy from her dance class. Kurt'

'Maybe I'll go talk to him then.'

'Why?'

Now it was Saul's turn to ignore his friend. He shrugged and changed the topic. 'Are you ready for practice?'

'Do you think you will be able to play?' Ezra asked and decided to go with the flow. He knew Saul well enough that pressing him further would be to no avail.

Saul took a quick step forward and stopped in front of Ezra. 'You think I can't?' Saul barked, raising his voice with each vowel. 'I'm still the captain of this team,' he said and tapped on Ezra's chest with his index finger.

'I didn't mean that,' Ezra said, failing to mask indignance in his voice and did not push away his friend's finger probing his chest. 'Coach will make that decision. You know very well that he's not always a sweetheart.'

***

'*Poppy would be in the classroom,*' Saul thought as he walked to Biology class, the last one before the football practice. As the dam holding back emotions and possibilities he could not process started to crack, questions and doubts began flooding his head. Saul fought back against the devastation inside him, if only to prevent tears. '*What if I walk to the classroom and see Poppy with someone else? What would I do? What can I do?*' he sighed and stopped in front of the classroom door. '*Should I just break up with her? We said nothing to each other.*' But he was afraid that if he opened his mouth, he would only muster enough will to gurgle, 'I love you' and 'Why did you kill Sophie?' It wasn't the time for the first and not the place for the latter.

Mrs. Gemma, the biology teacher, walked by Saul, tapped on his shoulder without a word, and entered the classroom. She was a ginger, well-built, and tall woman who effused an aura of military authority until she started speaking to reveal her bubbly, soft personality. Mrs. Gemma and her inspiring attitude was one reason Saul had decided to study biology.

He took a deep breath and walked in right after her. He didn't raise his eyes from the floor tiles and passed by Poppy's desk. Honey-infused perfume tingled his nose, but he didn't take a deep breath to enjoy the scent for fear of being over-whelmed further. '*How strange!*' he thought. '*even a subtle scent flashes more memories before our eyes compared to a sharp image or a clear sound.*' He closed his eyes momentarily and felt Poppy's warm breath linger over his face again. He opened his eyes to see the back of Poppy's head. '*How close yet so far.*'

'Today, we are going to learn about reproduction systems, ' Mrs. Gemma said and dropped her books with a thud on the table.

'I can give you some private lessons,' a boy sitting on the front row whispered, louder than intended, in an unfortunate moment of silence in the classroom, to the girl sitting next to him.

'Keep harassing her, and I'll give *you* a lesson,' the teacher warned and waved the chalk in her hand towards the boy. The class laughed along with the chastised boy, who looked like he wouldn't mind an extra lesson from her. The girl sitting next to him blushed slightly and tugged strings of her dark blond hair; she seemed interested in private lessons, for which details were to be ironed out after the class. Saul looked at Poppy laughing and realized life was going on, with or without him. He could not laugh along, not because he didn't find the interchange funny but he felt alienated from everyone, especially himself. Then his soul became separated from his body, and he started watching the class from the ceiling. '*How do I recall certain memories from the third perspective?*' he thought. He was sure to remember this moment also, alas bitterly.

'What is the meaning of life?' Mrs. Gemma asked the class and started pacing around the desks.

'Having sex with as many partners as possible. That's what all animals try to do,' said another boy, and the rest of the class giggled again.

Mrs. Gemma shook her head in annoyance and walked back to her desk. 'I see that we have multiple jokers in the class,' she said and tapped on her desk. 'You are all hoping to graduate next month. Do *not* make me go talk to Mrs. Pallas for a different arrangement.'

The class fell silent as Mrs. Gemma's threat and authority, borrowed from the counselor, subdued the rising raucousness in the class. The purpose of life, from the biological perspective, is to stay alive. Be immortal.' She then walked to the blackboard, drew a squiggly circle, and titled it 'cell.'

'Think of this humble cell. Building block of organisms. Even it is coded to stay alive and live forever. However, after a certain time, it decays,' she said and crossed out the cell with chalk. 'What can our cell do then?' she asked and turned back to the classroom.

'Produce off-spring.' Saul answered.

'Yes. If you pass on your genes, you achieve the closest status possible to immortality. This desire drives every being.'

Saul raised his hand and even established brief eye contact with Mrs. Gemma. She then ignored him and asked everyone to open their books to 'reproductive systems.' Saul realized he had tried to raise his non-existing hand, then chuckled at his mistake.

'Do individual worker bees or ants have the same genes or DNA? The same one with the queen bee?' he asked and raised his right hand this time.

She thought for a moment and stared outside the window as if expecting a bee to fly in and buzz the answer to her ear.

'No, they don't. A worker bee is born from an unfertilized egg from a queen bee. Why?'

'Then they are not seeking immortality. They can't pass on their genes, as only a queen bee produces offspring. What is the point of the existence of worker bees, then?'

Mrs. Gemma clapped her hands and smiled from ear to ear. 'What a great observation.' She looked around the classroom, but none of the students seemed to understand or appreciate the logic behind the inquiry. Students like Saul made teaching worth all the effort. 'Does anyone have an answer to that?' she asked, knowing no one would try. It was the last class on a summer Friday, and these students were all seniors. So nearly all of them already were thinking about what they were going to do after the class; Poppy was going to buy a new dress for the prom, the girl sitting in the front dreamt about the private 'lessons,' Mrs. Gemma herself thought about going to the city park for a stroll, and Saul wanted to learn about Sophie. Seeing no one else was attempting to answer her, the teacher peeled herself away from the sunny weather outside and went on to an explanation:

'Good questions. Somewhere in the evolution, bees must have realized they had to concede their individuality to survive as a species. Hive trumps the individual bee.' She then drew a human figure on the board. 'Another comparison would be our bodies. For example, not all of our cells are identical. But your stomach does not try to go on its way and split into other stomach copies. Our collective cells came into an agreement that they can only survive together, and to the next generation, they will transfer only part of their genes.' She nodded again, satisfied with her answer. 'Bees' reproduction system is very interesting. Two pages on bee reproduction for next week.'

A boy in the front row moaned loud enough to make himself heard and hissed, 'Idiot.' Saul knew he was being called out, so he sprang to his feet and went to the boy's desk.

'Don't write it then, idiot!' Saul said, slamming his fist on the desk, sending a pencil up in the air, and pushing the guy who did not deign to look back at Saul.

As Saul readied himself to land the next punch on the boy's smug face, Ezra pulled him back just in time.

***

Saul knocked on the salon's door, but the loud music booming inside indicated him not to expect anyone to invite him in. He opened the door and walked in with small steps. In the salon, ten couples were swirling with an invigorating yet soft Salsa tune. The instructor, a slender man in his forties, threw Saul a glance but decided not to bother with the intruder.

'Now we're going to practice the final combination,' the instructor said and asked the girl closest to him to be his partner. Facing one another, they held each other's crossed hands, the right on top, and started swaying back and forth. At count three, the instructor gave the girl a right turn, then they switched their crossed hands, looped their crossed arms over their heads, and the girl turned right one last time.

Although couples confirmed they understood the routine, most of them had blank expressions, revealing they weren't sure of themselves. Once the music started and couples twirled around trying to replicate the routine, the shortcomings of the dancers immediately became apparent. Some couples had mixed up their hands and ended up with weird locks. One poor guy who seemed confused was being chastised by his partner, who tapped her foot on the floor repeatedly and pointed to the single couple who managed to replicate the instructor who was now shouting, 'I said right hand on top' to a hapless awkward couple.

'*I should have come here with Poppy,*' Saul thought as an expanding regret took over him. '*I'll never be able to dance with Poppy. Or any other girl.*' He took another look at his arm. He wanted to run away, go back home, and cry himself to sleep. He would have given whatever was left of his life to re-live one happy, maybe even mediocre, day from the past. He fought the urge to run up to the wall and smash his head, but he couldn't help but clench his jaw until his teeth hurt. '*I need to learn what happened to Sophie,*' he thought. That was what kept him going.

***

As the dancers finished their last moves, Saul approached a girl and asked for Kurt. She pointed to a tall, slender guy with a non-remarkable face, one of thousands you would pass by every day and not notice or could not describe later on. If Saul hadn't already seen him dancing confidently and elegantly, Saul would have expected him to wobble like a newborn giraffe snuggling up to the legs of his mother.

'Are you Kurt?'

'What do you want?'

'I wanted to ask you something.'

'I am running late, get to it,' Kurt huffed and rolled his eyes. Saul tried to ignore his attitude, but the condescending pressed lips on the dancer's face were hard to swallow. Saul wanted to smash his non-remarkable face into the mirror of the salon but guessed it would be much harder to get any information from a corpse as he had not mastered necromancy yet.

'Mrs. Pallas sent me. I can go tell her that you didn't have time.' Saul said and gestured to leave towards the door.

'Wait!' Kurt said and grabbed Saul by his shoulder. 'What is it? It's been a long day. Excuse my grumpiness.' Saul took another look at Kurt's face, which now flashed with worry. He congratulated himself for the quick thinking on his feet in bringing up the counselor's name. He couldn't figure out what Sophie saw in this guy.

'We're doing research on why people kill themselves. You were dating Sophie, right?' Saul asked. Kurt nodded to confirm.

'Why did she kill herself, Kurt?'

Kurt looked puzzled and scratched his head. 'I have no idea. She didn't tell me anything.'

'Weren't you guys dating? How could you not know?' Saul pressed Kurt, but he could not help but think of Poppy. How much did he know about her, who she really was? Still, he kept asking, 'This research is really important. Mrs. Pallas and I would appreciate any help.'

'We broke up two months ago. She told me she was seeing someone else and broke up with me. I have to go now,' Kurt said and stepped around Saul to the door. Even Mrs. Pallas's name had its limits.

***

As Saul tied his shoes, he tried to make small talk with his teammates about the upcoming matches, but their curt replies didn't leave enough wiggle room for the conversation to carry on. The team dressed in silence and headed to the pitch together. '*I'll go easy.*' Saul thought. '*I haven't been running or practicing for two weeks. I need to warm up.*' After he jogged a bit to loosen his legs, he turned around to see why their coach was whistling, then saw that the coach was calling him over.

'Do you think you'll still be able to play?'

'That's why I am here,' Saul puffed up his chest. 'Did we start playing basketball, coach?'

'You must be out of shape. I don't think you can handle the fight inside the pitch anymore,' the coach said and pointed towards Saul's side with a neutral expression. Saul knew the coach only cared about his performance and how he was going to contribute to the team, so he couldn't get angry with the coach.

'Give me a chance, coach. Please. I deserve it.'

'Fine. I will substitute you in,' The coach said and whistled again to start the practice.

***

In the second half of the practice match, Saul joined the winning team. By now, he had realized that while running, he was struggling to balance himself as his center of gravity had shifted because of the missing arm, and he could only swing the right one to gain his balance during the sprints and turns. 'I'll get used to it,' he repeated to himself. 'I just need a bit of time. I'm still the captain of this team.'

Ezra crossed the ball to Saul, who caught it near the left corner of the opposition's box. He juggled the ball from right to left to size up the defender facing him. Saul had dribbled past him countless times before, but now he was going to play it safe. He pulled the ball to his right and bent it towards the top left corner of the goal.

A slight miss just over the crossbar. Saul cursed under his breath. His aim was off as he had lost his balance.

He tackled a midfielder in the center and sprinted across the field. The disgruntled midfielder caught up with him and tried to shoulder Saul off-balance. Even to his surprise, Saul maintained his balance and dribbled past him. Or so he thought. The guy then tackled him from behind. Saul instinctively tried to cushion the fall with his left arm, which had been torn apart by the now-dead tiger. Instead, Saul softened the impact of the grass with his face. He immediately started tasting his own blood in his mouth. Ezra lifted him up and carried him off the pitch.

***

'Let me look at it,' Daisy said and tried to lower Saul's hand down to see his nose.

The doctor said it'll be okay. Stop bothering me,' he said and pushed his mother's hand away. Daisy gave up on insisting further and threw herself on the bed next to Saul, tied her hands on her lap, and stared at the carpet.

'I'm worried about you, Saul,' Daisy said, fighting against her tears. 'You have to be careful...'

'Don't!' Saul said, jumping to his feet and pointing his index finger at himself. 'Do you want to pickle me in a jar and keep me in a cupboard?' He started yelling, 'I can look after myself!' His swollen and bruised face and the splint on his nose put his claim in doubt. His eyes were almost popping out from their sockets, along with veins on his face, almost protruding out from his skin.

'I'm sorry,' Daisy said, losing the fight against her tears. She stood up and headed towards the door. 'It's all my fault. You would have been better without me. Your father and sister would have been here too.' Daisy closed the door behind her without a noise.

Now Saul and his rage were alone in the room. He threw his chair to the wall, kicked a box full of books, which hurt his toes, and slammed his only fist on the desk. He was angry with himself, Poppy, Alice, Mrs. Pallas, the tiger, and the rest of the living beings. But not with Daisy, who just had to endure his discontent. Pain in his fingers and toes, increasing with time as the heat of the moment passed, pulled back Saul to face what he'd done. Nearly dislocating the door of his room from its hinges, he opened the door and sprinted back after his mom to collapse at her feet and ask for forgiveness. 'None of this is your fault. It's all my doing. Forgive me.'

***

Another Monday with Mr. Lewis in the 'Suicide Philosophy' class. No props this time. He walked in and collected their homework assigned three weeks ago on 'Aristotelian view of suicide and its impact on the state.' Saul did not understand why Athenians did not forgive Socrates, why the philosopher drank the hemlock, and why Poppy let Sophie die.

'Ancient people, our ancestors, had peculiar and most of the time conflicting views of suicide. While they venerated the martyrdom of a soldier sacrificing himself, they condemned the individual and the personal cause leading to suicide,' Mr. Lewis said and began touring the class. Saul could not help but think how the teacher had planned to kill himself. He must have surely dedicated a lot of time to research the best method. '*Would it not be ironically funny if he had a sudden heart attack or got crushed under the wheels of a car?*' Saul thought and chuckled to himself, which drew the ire of Mr. Lewis, who reasonably took the gesture as a mockery of his statement.

'Do you find states' infringement on personal liberties risible, Saul?' Mr. Lewis asked and leaned over Saul's desk.

'No, sir.' Saul said and kept staring at his desk. Half fearing to face Mr. Lewis, half fearing to fall into a laughter fit that would make the reaction even harder to explain. Content with the submissive attitude he received, Mr. Lewis continued with the lecture:

'It might come as absurd to you, but in other societies throughout history, even people facing a death sentence were not given the option to take their own life. In Ancient Athens, anyone planning to commit suicide had to ask for the permission of the state as suicide was a privilege granted to few.'

'What punishment can be given to a person who has committed suicide? Are they punished if they are found alive?' the scrawny ginger kid asked.

'A valid question. There used to be societies that prosecuted people whose suicide attempts failed. But there were also other laws for the ones who succeeded. Their bodies were dragged through the streets as a humiliation to their loved ones. Their families lost their right to inherit the estate or titles that otherwise would have been passed upon them.'

The class shook their heads in unison to disapprove of the cruelty of the previous generations. Saul looked at Poppy sitting a couple desks away. She was taking notes from what Mr. Lewis said. Saul wondered what she found useful to write. 'Suicide is a privilege granted to few. Don't drag their bodies; let their families inherit the gold.'

'Class, today we are going to talk about the romanticization of suicide in Shakespeare's plays from Othello to Romeo and Juliet.'

***

Today, Saul's meeting with Mrs. Pallas was after Mr. Lewis' class. He knocked on the open door and entered without waiting for an invitation. She did not lift her head to greet or acknowledge Saul. He again felt a ghost pain crushing his arm and breaking his long-gone bones. Under his shirt sleeve, he pulled the sock over his stump and massaged it to remind his brain what had happened.

'I was going over your homework for Mr. Lewis' class, the one about Achilles and Ajax. You called both of their ends needless, and you introduced the concept of 'social suicide,' which you defined as the collection of external factors in a community that forces an individual to kill themselves,' Mrs. Pallas said and raised her head to look at the student sitting across her. 'Your arguments through the paper were consistent; thus, you have received a high mark.'

Saul briefly closed his eyes. Whenever he felt down when he was little, his sister would tell him to escape to a happy moment in the past. As he searched for a memory to bring momentary bliss to this room, he found all of his former happy places were charred beyond salvation. He couldn't stand those involving his sister or Poppy. He tried to bring his sister's face before his eyes, but the harder he concentrated, the blurrier she got. For a very long time, she didn't visit his dreams either. He would even have settled for a nightmare. He had to contend with Sophie and Alice, who made the only appearances in his nightmares.

'Your coach asked me to inform you that you are no longer the captain, and you have been subsequently removed from the team,' the counselor added, undeterred by silence and Saul's stoic expression. He opened his eyes and lifted his head to catch a glimpse of the spider leg fingers adorned by oversized rings. When their eyes met, Saul realized she also did not wear a particular expression.

'You're not speaking, Saul.'

'You didn't ask me a question.'

She then leaned back in the chair and crossed her arms. Saul slightly shifted forward and ran his fingers through his hair. His arm had stopped hurting, but he felt the pain had shifted to his heart, which picked up pace with every beat.

'You're understandably upset for breaking up with Poppy.'

'It's none of your business.'

'You know that I have to write letters of recommendation to universities that you are worthy of higher education,' the counselor said as her lips arched upwards far enough to displace an ant and a ringed finger tapped on a pile of papers on the table. 'We do not blindly value only knowledge and hard work in our society but care for others.'

'Is that why you let Sophie die?' Saul said and cursed under his breath as his voice broke. He closed his eyes and tried to regain his composure. Veiled threats of denying his school application had lost their effect on him. He asked the question that was burning his brain so his soul might get freed from its shackles. 'I beg you,' Saul muttered, placing his fist on his heart and leaning forward. Any further and he would have fallen on his knees. 'Why did Sophie kill herself? It eats me up.'

'I told you that there are no easy answers. What do you want to hear?' Mrs. Pallas said and made herself more comfortable in the chair. She displaced another ant upwards with her lips.

'You know what bothered her!' Saul yelled, jumping to his feet and punching his fist on the counselor's table, toppling the pile of applications. 'You're just deeply disturbed.' He paused for a moment to gather his thoughts and, if possible, stop a mental train from derailing. 'Just because no one loves you, it's not fair to take it out on other people.'

'Ha!' the counselor exhaled and straightened her posture. She then dropped her shoulders down and put her elbows on the armchair, as she knew Saul was now between her claws. She had all she needed to deny him his fortune, whether or not he was aware. 'Look at yourself. Do you think you will gather throngs of admirers? Half a man!'

'Cut it out!' Saul yelled once more and threw the papers to the floor. 'If that's so great, why don't you kill yourself already?'

'Funny, you are obsessed with Sophie now. Regret must be really eating you up for not asking her why,' she said and remained oblivious to Saul's anger or him trashing the room. 'Just because your sister left a note, you think you know why she killed herself.' The counselor chuckled and crossed her arms. 'Leave the room at once.'

'Don't bring her into this.'

'I was her teacher as well. A remarkable girl,' the counselor continued, well aware she didn't need to veil her contempt for Saul. 'I went to the same school with your mother. Sad to see she is losing both of her children. Let's see what will happen to her. Now, leave the room!' she said, stood up, and pointed the door. Mrs. Pallas was planning to notify the headmaster to sever Saul's relationship with the school. Although Saul was indeed going to be dismissed from the school, it was not for the reasons she had intended.

Saul jumped on the table and kicked Mrs. Pallas in her face. Upon contact with Saul's shin, Mrs. Pallas's lower lip blasted open, squirting blood. Her jaw was dislocated, and four of her teeth flew out. The force of the impact caused her to lose her balance, fall from the chair, and hit her head on the wall, which caused a minor concussion. Saul jumped down from the table and grabbed her by the throat. She caught Saul by his wrist but could not exert enough force to change the course of events as he rammed her head once more against the wall. Following the second hit, gravity pulled her hand down as her body went limp. No apparent physical damage was on the wall, which showed that it was a load-bearing wall, not a curtain wall, which would have caved in. The only damage to the wall was blood stains that slowly dripped down, which would be cleaned the following day with bleach. After the fourth hit, two students came into the room and pulled Saul away.

Part 5

The cell was much brighter and spacious than he had dreaded it would be. Windows, big enough that he could have easily walked through without crouching, revealed an idyllic summer scene around the lake and surrounding rolling woods outside the prison. If it was not for the rather chilly temperature inside, Saul could have imagined himself lying on the dry grass with a constant tickling sensation of ants running over his skin. The cell included two single beds, separated by seven steps, twin chairs, drawers, and a partly open door that gave way to a small sink, a squat toilet, and a shower head. A tall man inside the bathroom was washing his hands. Saul could only see the back of his new cellmate, who had curly hair streaked with white.

He threw himself and his bag over the bed that was pointed to by the guard, who walked back to the thick glass door of the cell and closed it with a soft thud that surprised Saul, who had expected a dramatic metallic clang sound to seal him off. Outside the glass walls of his cell was a circular prison with three floors, each housing thirty glass-door cells facing each other on every floor. In the center of the floor was a three-storied glass tower housing the guards who were behind their desks or walking around with papers in their hands.

'I have to escape.' Saul decided and crossed out some questions in his mind. 'Why' was clear to him. Neither he nor Daisy could have survived while Saul was stuck in this glass jar for a long time. 'When' was also rather obvious: at the first opportune moment. 'How' was not clear yet. He knew he shouldn't even attempt to smash the glass, didn't think he could dig a tunnel, and outside help was unlikely from his mother, even though he guessed she would have definitely tried. 'To where' was another question that had to be answered. Following the escape and the potential chase, he was going to run back to his home and pick up his mother. A fugitive's life seemed the only option after that. He was willing to suffer through it, but did he have the right to drag Daisy into another calamity? Maybe she would pick up the phone and call the police. 'Forgive me, Saul. It is the best thing to do for both of us.' No, he decided. Although his mother was indeed a law-abiding citizen, she wouldn't call the cops on him. But did he have the right to upend her life, and what could he offer her? How would they survive if Daisy had an illness? Which hospital would accept them and not turn both of them in to the cops? Then, she would also be in jail. He had to run away alone. Drop a note to her house. 'I'm okay. I love you.' Where would he go, and how would he survive without a job, money, or even food? After the deliberation, he erased the 'why' and 'when' questions from his mind. He was now filled with doubts about himself, his mother, and the rest of the universe.

When the judge asked him whether he felt remorse, he said 'Yes.' He didn't necessarily regret what he did to Mrs. Pallas but to himself, Sophie, Poppy, Abraham, his sister, and everyone else on the planet who had to endure the torture. 'Yes, your honor. I do.' All the troubles in his mind during the day and unconsciously in his nightmares at night were distilled into an obsession with Sophie. '*If only I knew what had happened to her, everything else would be magically fixed*,' he believed, though never admitted openly. Whenever he imagined Sophie killing herself because of an incurable disease, he felt the burden off his shoulders. 'I couldn't have done anything,' but in the darker corners of his mind, another Sophie lurked who was killing herself out of loneliness, and a friend would have sufficed to tie her to his world. Tides once again turned in his mind: '*I have to escape*' as he drowned in the middle of a sea of remorse and pain.

The new cellmate turned off the faucet, and the running water finally stopped beating the marble. When the cellmate stepped outside the bathroom, Saul was struck by the most beautiful face, with sharp features borrowed from a statue of an ancient god whom Saul remembered seeing on a school trip a long time ago. As the cellmate dried his hands, Saul noticed that the inmate's hands were gradually whiter than the rest of his arms, which were connected to the body of a possible marathon runner. Two signs of life that radiated from the sculpture, apart from its motion, were the energetic hazel eyes running all around Saul and a light stubble adding to the charisma of the pseudo-Greek god.

Saul rose from the bed and gestured to shake hands but was refused.

'I do not shake hands'

'As you wish.' Saul mumbled and dropped back to the bed.

'The rope is in the drawer, and the hook is there,' Saul's cellmate pointed to the ceiling. 'Make sure you position the noose in front of your left ear.' he said and hung his towel behind the bathroom door. Saul took a couple seconds to process what his cellmate had suggested, then jumped towards the guy, gripped his collar and started yelling, 'I'm not going to...'

With a swift hit and twist to Saul's wrist, the guy broke off the young boy's grip and pushed Saul back onto the bed. 'Good for you. I just don't want an idiot who doesn't know how to hang himself struggling for minutes to die.' He then fixed his collar, threw a disgusted and tired look at his hands, and went back to the sink to wash them again. 'As you would imagine, it is rather unpleasant and distracting.'

Saul opened and closed his mouth several times but sufficed with exhaling angrily.

'Benjamin,' the guy revealed his name from the bathroom while scrubbing his palms with his nails.

'Saul,' he replied after a moment of hesitation. But quickly concluded that it was no use antagonizing his cellmate if he wanted to sleep with some peace of mind.

'Nice to meet you, Saul.'

'Likewise, Ben'

'It's Benjamin'

***

Three days passed, and everyone, dead or alive, arrived on a Wednesday morning. Saul was looking at the glass guard tower, expecting one of its doors to open so a guardian could come to pick him up to meet his mother. He hadn't talked to her almost for a week, and now he felt blisters opening in his heart. In biology class, they had learned that the heart tissue never regenerates, 'such a shame.'

He wished last week was a complete blur in his mind, but it was as vivid as the moment he had kissed Poppy for the first time. When he closed his eyes, he could still feel her warm breath lingering over his face and her eyelashes fluttering on his cheek. With the same intensity of the memory of the first kiss, he lived through getting used to the cold steel of handcuffs, rebellious then regretful admission of guilt, and phoning his mother for the first time to say sorry. He had looked forward to seeing Daisy, but now he did not want the time to come, as it would pass by very quickly. There was more pleasure and comfort in keeping the dream within arm's reach for a later moment but not grasping it.

'Are you worried about the guards watching over you?' Benjamin interrupted Saul's inner monologue and pointed to the glass tower of the guards who were running around it carrying papers and passing them to each other.

'I'm not doing anything. Why would I be worried?' Saul shrugged and looked at Benjamin, who had decided to shave today. 'Also, I can see that they're not watching.'

'But you can only be sure that they're not watching as long as you keep your eyes on the tower,' Benjamin chuckled, sat upright on his chair, and picked up the morning newspaper: 'CORRUPTION REVEALED: Minister Embezzled Millions Meant for the Schools'

'Then they shouldn't have made the guard tower out of glass. The guards should only be able to see us.'

Benjamin laughed and lowered the newspaper to peek at Saul. 'But how are the guards going to be supervised to make sure they're watching us?' He then flipped to the next page: 'SMALLPOX ELIMINATED.' 'It's a perfect design. Both us and guards need to assume we're being watched at all times and act accordingly.'

'Wouldn't this mean they are prisoners here too?' Saul asked. He was admittedly bothered by Benjamin's nonchalant attitude toward everything. Even though Saul could not see Benjamin's face because the newspaper veiled it, he would have sworn that Benjamin was smiling to himself for putting Saul down.

'No, don't simplify it.' Benjamin said, chuckling, confirming the suspicion about his mood. 'I'm just saying it's a good design.' He then lowered the newspaper, locked his eyes on Saul, and leaned over as if someone was eavesdropping, 'But let me tell you a secret. Neither we nor them care what the other is doing, as much as our counterpart thinks we do. That is the ingenuity of the system here.'

A glass door on the ground floor of the tower opened, and a guard marched towards their cell.

***

The terrace of the prison overlooked a serpentine lake with families and couples rowing on hourly rented small boats. Saul had not heard of the lake before. It mattered little now. The terrace was filled with pots of orchids, roses, petunias, and lavender, buzzing with honey bees. 'Guards must be keeping hives nearby.' Saul guessed.

He sat across from his mother, and guards served them freshly brewed tea and gave them privacy in a corner. 'You have thirty minutes'

As he sat down on the soft garden chair, he cursed under his breath as he sank too comfortably for his taste and the occasion. '*Thirty minutes, how short,*' Saul thought. He didn't know how much would be enough or considered long. It was never going to get easier to say 'farewell.'

A courtesy game began to mark their half-hour alone, a conversation dotted with flowers, bees, and the humid weather. He wished he hadn't noticed the deepening of crow's feet around her eyes, which were becoming more translucent yet not revealing more of her or whatever was left. Small movements caught his heart in wrench; Daisy taking a little more time to walk, her lips arching less with a smile and her shoulders dropping more.

'The counselor is in a coma; she didn't sign a euthanasia authorization, so she still has a full month to wake up before the grace period ends.' Daisy swerved into uncharted territory as the first five minutes passed with courteous necessities. Saul responded with a shrug. Daisy believed that if Mrs. Pallas woke up, she could forgive Saul, and the judge could drastically reduce, maybe even completely lift, the thirty-year prison sentence. Saul thought that if the counselor woke up, she would ask for a harsher punishment. A ray of sunlight pierced his eye, causing a burning sensation on his iris. But he didn't tilt his head away because he accepted and even relished these minor daily irritations as part of his deserved punishment for the misfortune he had brought on Daisy and himself.

Reading Saul's empty stare as he gazed over the lake, Daisy swerved back into the comfort of chit-chat. 'They called me last Thursday while you were waiting to get transferred here and asked if I wanted to make an appointment for Wednesday,' she said, pulling her chair closer to Saul and holding his hand. 'I told them that I would come every Wednesday, but they insist I must call on Thursdays to make an appointment each week.' Saul leaned over and picked up his cup of tea. A hint of bergamot tickled his nose.

'The counselor said you two went to the same high school.'

'Really? I don't remember her.'

Saul replaced his cup and buried his hands in his palm. Daisy stood up from her chair and pulled him to her bosom.

'I'm sorry, Mom. For everything,' he started weeping.

'Don't. We will get through this. Together,' she said and ran her nails through his hair.

The guards gave them an extra five minutes to embrace.

***

While lying in his bed, Saul read through the letter Ezra had sent. He didn't know his friend had such neat cursive handwriting, just maybe slightly smaller than Saul would have preferred. Saul folded the letter along the original lines, inserted it in the envelope, and placed it on the top shelf of the drawer. '*Is Poppy happy that she abandoned a sinking ship just at the right moment?*' Saul wondered. '*Probably she doesn't think about me at all.*' He then rolled over to face the wall and ran his finger through the wrinkled turquoise waves of the wall's surface. '*I have to escape. I have to find out what had happened to Sophie.*'

'How was your mother?' Benjamin said as he turned off the faucet.

'You know, she tries to keep her spirits up.'

'Why are you here, Saul?'

'I ended up in a fight. How about you?' Saul replied as he quickly realized that attacking a middle-aged lady would not act as a social lubricant to make friends. But he countered the idea by mentally noting to himself that Benjamin was not here in the cell with him as a punishment for his excessive good deeds. He rolled over and sat on the edge of the bed, facing Benjamin.

'I guess it was after you saved the girl.' Benjamin chuckled and hung up his towel, ending another ten minutes of hand scrubbing, which left his hands even whiter. 'Don't be surprised.' Benjamin laughed again at Saul opening and closing his mouth like a fish plucked out of the sea. 'You were all over the newspapers.'

'Well, it was after that. But I couldn't save the girl. She killed herself shortly after due to scars the tiger had left,' Saul said, shifting to a sitting position and folding his hands on his lap.

'Irrelevant,' Benjamin said and laid down on the bed facing Saul. 'I don't think it was the scars, but anyway. Do you think she had committed suicide by jumping into the cage in the first place?'

'No way,' Saul shrugged. The sun was setting outside their window and rising in some other part of the world. Shapes were becoming blurred as the curtain of twilight dropped. The orange of the skyline reminded Saul of the tiger's fur. His stump hurt again, and he let out a groan. 'She slipped and fell. You need to be crazy to do that.'

Benjamin fell into a fit of laughter. 'How...' He attempted, but he could not gain his composure. 'How...' Benjamin started again and wiped tears from his eyes, or pretended to. 'How do sane people kill themselves, Saul?' He then rose from his bed and sat next to Saul, who felt uncomfortable but did not flinch. Benjamin now grew serious about the topic at hand, which Saul thought was not really a laughing matter mere seconds ago, either. 'Does a father hang himself in the living room so his children can wake up to find him in the morning? Does a lover simply leave a note to her boyfriend and head to the nearest bridge or train tracks?' Benjamin said as his voice raised with each vowel, each intonation. 'How do sane people kill themselves, Saul?' Benjamin put his hand on Saul's shoulder blade to turn him. 'Were you going to leave her if you knew she was indeed trying to get herself killed?'

The dinner bell rang, and guards started opening the doors of the cells. Two by two, occupants of each cell lined up in front of their door, then the flock marched around the tower to the corridor connecting to the cafeteria in another building. As they turned around the guards' tower, in the cell next to the corridor, a middle-aged man stepped on the chair in his room and hung the rope to the hook in the ceiling. After adjusting the noose behind his neck, he kicked his chair beneath his feet. Saul saw the inmate's round face switch between shades of red and purple while his feet violently rubbed against each other. Then he clawed the noose with both hands. The absurdity of the scene was heightened by the growing bulge poking out from the inmate's crotch. As the inmate kept struggling, others continued on their march to the cafeteria, discussing what was going to be for dinner that night. 'They'd better not serve peas again,' a stocky guy moaned to one of the female guards, who responded with a shrug and pointed him to the corridor.

'See, I told you. He should have positioned the noose in front of his left ear.' Benjamin pulled Saul back as the latter took a step toward the cell and pointed to the still-struggling man. Saul wondered whether the inmate now regretted his decision as sweat condensed on the man's brow. 'The guards must also be annoyed to be late to their dinner,' Benjamin added and pushed away a guy who stepped on his foot. 'Watch where you're going, punk.'

***

Ten minutes after Saul sat down for dinner–peas with mashed potatoes–the guards who were left behind to watch over the man walked into the cafeteria and joined their colleagues having dinner upstairs.

Benjamin glanced over a newspaper left open: "PUBLIC SUPPORT MAXIMUM FOR THE REFERENDUM: CAMPAIGN STARTED TO INCREASE TURNOUT." He then pushed it off the table with his elbow.

'Feeling sad that you are not going to partake in history?' Saul grinned. Benjamin grew serious as his eyes furiously rolled in their sockets, trying to unleash themselves on Saul.

'That referendum will fail. Mark my words.' Benjamin tapped the edge of his knife on the table. 'It will be the first domino to bring down the invisible tyranny. They're not going to denigrate the sanctity of life any further. I will not allow it.' Saul was taken aback by his cellmate's heated reaction.

'If that referendum had passed a year ago, I would have been in jail even earlier,' Saul said. He then wondered whether he would have saved Sophie by risking prosecution. Would she have pressed charges against him? *This one officer. He was the one that saved me. I want justice.*

'Me too, Saul. Me too.'

'You didn't tell me why you are here, Benjamin,' Saul said after burying leftover peas in the mashed potatoes. He was struggling to get rid of the imagery of two feet rubbing against each other, now overlapping with Sophie approaching the cliff.

'Neither did you, Saul,' Benjamin shot back and reached for a glass of water. 'Driest mashed potatoes I have ever eaten.' An inmate came towards them to sit next to Benjamin but ended up getting chased away.

'Go sit somewhere else.'

'Why? Anyone else sitting here?' the meek, bespectacled guy asked. He stopped in his tracks with his tray in his hand, slightly hunched over, ready to sit.

'Yes. My imaginary friend. Shoo.' Benjamin gestured him away and gulped down the glass of water. Deciding it was not a battle he neither wanted to win nor fight, the bespectacled guy sighed and kept on looking for another seat. Benjamin threw his utensils on the tray, pushed it to the side, and leaned forward to Saul. 'I was in the central station to catch a commuter rail,' he began his story. Saul couldn't help but think that Benjamin's mannerisms and attitude, contradicting his clean features, made him primally disturbing. A beautiful sonata ruined by an off-chord violin. 'In the corner of my eye, I caught a young guy swinging back and forth, cursing under his breath. Clearly distressed, you see. As one train passes by the platform, he sprints to throw himself under.' Benjamin said while imitating a guy running with his fingers on the table. As soon as the finger figure put his right leg off the table, Benjamin's left hand caught him in the air.

'People were furious with you because you stopped him, then,' Saul said and bobbed his head up and down.

'No way! They were grateful.'

'I don't believe that.'

'Are you calling me a liar?' Benjamin slammed his fist on the table, sent three peas flying off the tray, and made two guards standing at the entrance put their hands on the batons strapped to their hips.

'I didn't mean... I...' Saul said. 'I was, you know...'

Benjamin stared a couple more seconds into Saul's eyes and laughed again. 'No worries. I'm messing with you. I missed laughing in here.' He then reached across the table to tap his cellmate's shoulder as a sign of camaraderie to release the tension.

'They weren't upset, because I saved their commute time. The guy's corpse would have delayed all of us for thirty minutes, at least. Waiting for the body to be scraped up and rails to be scrubbed.' Upon seeing the issue between the prisoners was resolved, the guards dropped their hands from their batons and resumed chatting among themselves: 'I should have stayed at school.' 'At least we're not them.'

Then, a 'Mr. Important' stepped from the group of people who gathered around us. "Why didn't you take the O-Train? I daresay the government is too easy on these delinquents. Too easy!"' Benjamin imitated the man in an alto voice and flailed his arms to put on airs.

'What's the O-train?' Saul asked as he finished off his dinner and pushed his tray aside. Inmates around them were getting more boisterous as everyone filled their stomachs. Saul always had imagined prisons as places of constant sorrow and desperation, which it was most of the time, but communal moments like meals provided a make-believe 'piazza' atmosphere as worries were momentarily dashed aside.

'People jumping on train tracks became a nuisance.' Benjamin picked up pace and reached for a toothpick as some inmates rose up from their tables and started heading back to their cells. 'So, they built a new train line, the O-train. It goes nowhere and just travels around in a circle so people can jump in front of it in designated areas.'

'Wrap up the meal, gentleman. Trays in the racks, please.' A guard's voice boomed from the speakers above.

As they were walking back to their cell in the stream of other inmates, Saul stepped aside and became separated from Benjamin to pass by the cell of the man who hanged himself before dinner. The cell was now cleaned, the bed fitted with fresh linen awaiting its next guest. The chair was back in its place next to the drawer, which probably housed a new rope. '*Do they provide a new rope?*' Saul thought. '*Most likely not, it would be a waste.*'

When he walked into the cell, he found Benjamin scrubbing his hands, so Saul sat down on the bed to wait his turn to use the bathroom, but knowing it would take a while, he made himself comfortable. 'What happened then?' Saul called out to the bathroom.

'Where was I?'

'Some guy was complaining.'

'The police came, reprehended the guy, and instructed him to go to the O-Train, of course, given that he still wanted to kill himself. The 'Mr. Important' kept badgering the young guy as the latter stumbled up the stairs. "Look at him, probably he's drunk or on other drugs."' Benjamin once again adopted the alto voice and started rinsing his hands. 'He then came to me and started complaining, complaining, and complaining. I asked him to keep his mouth shut, but no. He went on about how those people, who are willing to cause disturbance to everyone, have no place in our society.' Benjamin said and finally stepped out of the bathroom, drying his hands on his towel. 'He then turned to me and said, "Is not that so?"'

Saul rose from his bed and approached the bathroom as his suddenly full bladder bested his curiosity.

'What then?' Saul asked as Benjamin fell silent to savor his inmate's curiosity and pretended to focus on his towel.

'I said no. And pushed him in front of the oncoming train.'

***

Wednesday once again arrived. Saul rolled inside the bed and kept quiet so as not to wake up his cellmate. He then clutched his stump and felt its end, which admittedly got better day by day. Even the ghost pain had significantly subsided. Every day inside the prison, his amputation was less of a problem, not simply because he got used to it, but there was not much need for two arms anyway: no one to hug, nowhere to climb, no opportunity to dance. He concluded that his problem was not that he was missing an arm but that he needed two arms, as everything outside was designed as such. He rolled over once again. '*Thirty years,*' he thought, '*A full lifetime for many. If I ever leave here, I'll be forty-eight.*' He started worrying about where he would go and how he would survive. He dozed off to sleep again. In his dream, he ran into Poppy in her forties, beautiful as ever, arms locked with Ezra, followed by two teenage kids. The couple greeted Saul with enthusiasm and asked him to stop by their house. 'Would you not like to meet Uncle Saul, kids?' Poppy asked. When the kids turned around, Saul saw himself and his sister.

He woke up from one nightmare to another and once again found himself in a prison cell. A wave of apathy had overtaken him; at least, that was what he had assumed. He cared less for the life outside, especially what they thought about him, apart from his mother, of course. *'She needs to let go of me and live her own life,'* Saul thought and rolled in his bed. *'I should tell my mother not to visit me again. But I couldn't live without her, so I condemn my mother to suffer under the pretense of love.'*

A letter slid through the opening of the door and landed softly on the ground. Another letter from Ezra. Saul picked up the letter but didn't care about the content, which was nothing to care about. His friend could have just sent an empty envelope with 'Thinking about you' scribbled on it. *'That would have been easier to reply to,'* Saul thought. He pondered about writing back to Ezra. *'I learned Sophie was seeing someone else. Who could it be? Is that why Sophie killed herself?'* Then he dreamed about getting a reply with an answer.

***

It was almost time to meet Daisy. 'I have to tell her not to visit me again,' Saul whispered to himself. 'Maybe it will break her heart at first, but she will survive. What if she doesn't survive and kill herself? Would I be happy that her suffering was over? Am I that important to her?' Saul lifted his eyes to the ceiling and caught his reflection in the shiny hook. He turned his eyes towards the bottom shelf of the drawer where Benjamin had said lay a rope. Saul did not open the drawer out of fear he couldn't resist the temptation that was rising in him each second. 'Did Sophie struggle as I do now? Looking for an exit that's not there? I'm sorry. It's all my fault. I have to let my mom live her life.'

Behind the steel bars, he heard the steps of the guards coming to deliver him to his mother.

***

Saul immediately wished he had gone blind so as not to see Daisy this way. *'How old can someone get in a week?'* he wondered as his eyes jumped from the deepening wrinkles on her hand to the beautiful turquoise gems almost buried behind the entrenched eye bags. Out of compassion, Saul wished she was dead. So Daisy would be relieved from her pain, and in return, he would be unleashed from his shackles. A whirl of guilt took over as he stepped closer to the chair under the sun, where they also sat last time.

'You didn't shave, baby.'

'Sorry, I'll do it next time,' Saul said, burying his face in Daisy's palms and kissing them a thousand times.

'Don't, baby. I like this too.' Daisy squeezed his chin.

After a chit-chat and two cups of bergamot-infused black tea, their time was already up. The less time left, the more things bottled up inside them, yearning to be released, but only a few ended up seeing daylight.

'I'm sorry, Saul, I didn't understand your suffering,' Daisy said, burying her face in her son's palms.

'Don't say that, Mom,' Saul tried to lift her head back up. 'I shouldn't have let her get under my skin. But... But I couldn't control myself when she mentioned your name. Don't visit me again. It is better for you,' Saul muttered, hoping she wouldn't hear what he said, but at the same time, he could relieve his conscience by fulfilling an obligation.

'I don't want to hear it again.' Daisy held his face in her palms and pulled him. 'I love you. Whatever happened, happened. We'll get over this together. I'll be beside you wherever you go.'

He looked over the terrace to the concrete floor below. '*Three floors down. Even in the best-case scenario, I'd break my leg and get shot before I could crawl out. The best-case scenario would be to die immediately. If it wasn't for my mother,*' Saul thought.

'I love you, Mom.'

***

As the attempt to sever his relationship with his mother (which Saul still believed would have been the best for her) failed, he found himself once again in a miserable state. The guards dropped him back at his cell, and the glass door once again closed with a soft thud. After the small break on the terrace, holding a bergamot-infused tea cup, basking under the sun, and sharing a touch with Daisy, Saul found it harder to adapt back to his cell. 'Maybe even the weekly appointments are part of the punishment. "Look at what you are missing. Taste the freedom a bit and go back to your cell."' Benumbed, Saul walked into the cell to find Benjamin, who kept on reading today's newspaper: 'RECORD EMPLOYMENT: Government Stimulus Package Boosts Local Economies.'

'Why do you care what's going on outside anymore?' Saul asked and threw himself on the bed, which shook his stomach and did not help with the bubbling nausea.

'Do you want me to stare at the wall and drive myself crazy?' Benjamin flipped to the next page: 'REDUCTION: Military Spending to be Reduced for the Consecutive Year.' How was your mother?'

'She's melting away in front of my eyes.' He wanted to sleep a bit, but the restlessness would not permit him to doze off without physically exhausting himself, which was not an easy task to accomplish by pacing inside the cell. Anyway, he was not going to relax even in his sleep, where Sophie regularly appeared, strumming a guitar and melting away as soon as Saul approached her. There were also occasional guest appearances by Poppy, who usually stood silent in a corner, face half covered by shade. 'I can't take it anymore.' Saul smashed the glass door and attracted the attention of the guards, who always waited for an escalation to happen before intervening. No point jumping into every single mental breakdown. Benjamin lowered the newspaper to his lap, hesitating whether to console Saul or ask him to zip it. 'Why they just don't kill us, Benjamin? I deserve it anyway.' Saul collapsed on the bed and retold what had happened, starting and ending with Sophie. When Saul finished and turned his head to Benjamin for absolution, the latter rose to his feet and knelt beside Saul.

'You know the story of Socrates, right? The city of Greece had condemned the philosopher to death by drinking hemlock.' Benjamin semi-whispered as if expecting guards in the glass tower to be eavesdropping.

'They wouldn't even kill him themselves. Not to get their hands dirty.'

'Exactly. Even if he refused to do so, they were going to tie him to a plank outside, leaving him to the mercy of the elements,' Benjamin said and crouched closer to Saul, his hand on Saul's knee. 'But that is not the topic at hand. You see, Socrates was given a chance to escape from prison.'

'Did they catch him and force him to drink the hemlock?' Saul asked, as his heart started picking up a faster rhythm for comfort.

'He refused to abscond when given the chance. Socrates argued that by living in the society up to the trial, he implicitly accepted its rules. Now, running away would be impossible for both him and his family. What do you think, Saul?'

'If he was cheated by them, would not the agreement be over?'

'I think so too,' Benjamin replied and shook his head. He leaped to his feet and now turned his back to Saul. 'Once the deal is broken, it's no longer binding for the other.'

'I want to get out,' Saul pleaded, barely preventing himself from dropping to his knees and kissing Benjamin's feet, which he stopped short of doing, not because of his pride but because of the watchful eyes of the guards.

'I can't tell you anything else. Do you want to take a leap of faith?'

'I do.'

***

'It's the law; you have to allow it.' Benjamin stamped his foot on the floor. 'Each and every prisoner has the right to self-determination regarding ways in which a person can end their life, given reasonable and humane requests.' He repeated the clause in the open penal code booklet in front of the prison warden. The warden's room was the only place in the compound with solid walls and doors. The warden took off his glasses, slumped back in his chair, and tapped his fingers on his bald head, which reflected the artificial light from the bulb above. Saul had been watching Benjamin argue with the warden back and forth in Saul's stead for the last half hour while the two guards idly waited in the corner to take the inmates back to their cells.

'It *is* the law, but you are just requesting us to process it very quickly. What day is it, boys?' he addressed one guard. 'Ha. It's Friday.' He then answered his own question. 'And your appointment is next Tuesday...' and he kept on tapping his bald head, maybe giving out a morse signal to the guards 'more.peas.for.dinner.'

'I know. I know.' Benjamin waved his hand, interrupting the warden, and shifted his weight in the chair. 'You know we've grown a strong bond,' and pointed to Saul. 'It shouldn't be too much of a hassle to add his signature to the petition.'

'Fine, Fine. You are not going to give me a break, anyway.' The warden gave up, leaned sideways to the drawer beneath his desk, almost tipping over under his weight, and shuffled through the petitions. 'Ah! Here.' He then reached out to a black pen and slid it to Saul with the petition 'Your name and signature please.'

Saul read the title: 'Request to jump down from the Memorial Observation Deck.'

***

They were to leave for the bridge before the break of dawn. Now, Saul was happy that he had nothing of sentimental value with him, as he would have needed to leave it behind. *'What now has sentimental value to me anywhere?'* He went through a mental list as the guards came to pick them up from their cell. *'Not the gifts I received from Poppy or my sister. They are irreversibly tainted. Even the gifts from my mom remind me of good days that are long gone and fill me with nothing but melancholy.'*

Benjamin and Saul stepped out of their cell and passed by the windows of other inmates. The prison's high circulation rate meant even in the two weeks Saul was there, many prisoners had come and gone, usually bruised around the neck, most in a coffin and occasionally confined inside a jar.

***

As the minivan carrying the prisoners and three guards sped through the slumber of the dawn, Saul fought against the inconvenient urge rising from his bladder, a familiar sensation that awakened with either a high intake of water or a rush of adrenaline in the moment, now, it was mostly the latter for him. He dreaded going past familiar buildings or streets for fear of losing his composure and starting to wail. He closed his eyes and thought of running back to Daisy.

Dense streets packed with people yielded to open fields, followed by woods lining the highway as they approached their destination. Saul's mind played a scene from Mr. Lewis's class about the fate of people jumping from bridges. 'If you don't die upon impact, you might drown with broken bones, unable to surface.' He shivered and convulsed while searching for respite in Benjamin, who seemed to be napping. Saul's mind drifted back to his mother. What was going to be their happily ever after? He decided not to dwell on the details for now. Once he surfaced, he was going to have a lot of time. Another scene emerged from the shadows of his worries: forming a triangle with his hands above his head to break the surface tension, but the water rips out his fingernails. He shuddered. The sun rose higher.

'Ben, Saul, do you have anything to give to anyone? Now is a good time,' the short but stout guard leaned over to see the prisoners sitting behind.

'It's *Benjamin*,' Saul's roommate hissed, waking up from his nap but without opening his eyes.

'As you wish, Benny,' the guard chuckled and turned back again to lower his window. 'By the way, we called and canceled your visitor. It was your mom, right?'

'What?' Saul shrieked and jumped up from his seat, hitting his head on the roof of the minivan. Benjamin reached out to him and squeezed his leg.

'She had made an appointment last Thursday for tomorrow.' Before they went over a speed bump, the guard smacked the driver over the back of his head. 'Slow down, you idiot.' Not an action that stood out as an example of high judgment. 'When we approved the petition on Thursday, we called and canceled her appointment.'

Saul started trembling and leaned over Benjamin, who held up his cellmate from collapsing.

'I need to go home,' Saul mumbled and shivered with a wave of possible scenarios.

'Shh. You will. I'm sorry. You will.'

'Keep apart, you lovebirds!'

***

The minivan pulled into the parking lot close to the observation deck. The guards slid open the door to let Saul and Benjamin out. The sun was still on its way up the sky, changing the color of the hills and lakes from crimson to pastel tones of green for the former and turquoise for the latter.

'Come on, boys.' The guards led them to the observation deck.

Apart from two early bird tourists out for a stroll, the memorial deck and woods surrounding it were empty. Urged by the guards and partially dragged by Benjamin, Saul shambled towards the observation deck. Between the occasional tears and plenty of fears clouding his vision, Saul realized they were across the waterfall where he had pulled back Sophie last summer before the smoldering campfires. Birds chirped along as they covered the fifty steps between them and the deck, looking down to a slice of a gorge carved from fairy tales, full of colorful flowers, small animals, princesses, and unhappy endings.

The pair, arm in arm, climbed up the wooden stairs of the observation deck with no railings, which posed a significant risk to careless tourists trying to take photos with their backs turned to the view of the waterfall, the valley, and the river down below. Trembling, Saul realized he was, in fact, brave enough to face the cliff before him. He felt a sliver of pride, knowing that he had at least saved Sophie from the potentially gruesome death by drowning that awaited them now. As he walked the last couple of steps to the edge, he expected to see a boat ready to fish them out of the water, dead or alive, and bring them to shore. But to his disappointment, there was none. He expected a cold gale to take over him but ended up facing a warm summer breeze.

'Excuse me, sir,' one of the tourists approached the guards who were waiting to hop off to their minivan, of course, after seeing the inmates disappear in the waters flowing down and not to surface again. At least until the mouth of the river, which opened to the sea. 'Can you take our photo please?' All five of them turned to the two tourists. One of the guards, a young man in his late twenties, reached for the camera extended by the bearded tourist.

'We're on official duty. We can't help you now,' the short guard caught the hand of the young one in mid-air.

'Too bad,' the tourist said.

The guards, on the wooden steps of the deck, turned their back to the tourists to face Saul and Benjamin, who were a step away from the edge.

'We don't have all day, boys. Come on, Benny.'

'I told you, it's *Benjamin*. We will not take any more of your time.' Benjamin smiled back at the short guard as the long-bearded tourist pulled out a hunting knife that had been hidden in his backpack.

The short guard saw the reflection of the sun on the metal right before it penetrated the side of his neck and tore open his jugular vein. He clasped his neck and gurgled out blood before dropping to his knees. Simultaneously, the second tourist, an athletic woman in her thirties, stabbed the second guard in his back four times in quick succession before he collapsed, vomiting blood. The young would-be photographer guard jumped forward before the butchers could get their hands and knives on him and tried to pull his gun. Seizing the opportunity, Benjamin covered the distance between himself and the last remaining guard and pounced over his prey. The guard took a side step and connected an uppercut to Benjamin's chin, effectively taking him out of the brawl. Pulling his handgun from the holster, the young man stepped on the deck to safeguard his back and took aim at Saul, who had stayed neutral up to that point, in a mixture of shock and fear. As Saul raised his only hand to seek mercy, the guard turned his attention to the knife-wielding assailants.

'Drop your knives! Or I'll shoot. Now!'

'Easy does it, boy' the woman lowered her knife while eyeing her partner.

'Quick, you too! Drop your knife. Now!' the guard then shot between the assailants to make good on his threat. Seeing no other option, the couple dropped their knives while Benjamin balanced himself on all fours.

'Stay down! You two, get down!' the guard ordered and shot between the couple once again, sending the grass flying around and startling the rabbits in the woods. As the scene unfavorably unraveled before his eyes, Saul wanted only one thing: to go back home. He took a discreet step towards the distracted guard and jumped on him. Noticing the movement at the last second, the guard turned towards Saul and took aim at his chest. Saul hit the guard's wrist with his right hand before the guard could shoot and then shouldered him off the edge of the observation deck.

A gunshot rang once in the air but missed its target, whatever it was. The prisoners and their accomplices did not hear a thing as the wind carried away any sound, be it a scream or a body hitting the water.

***

'We weren't expecting a third guard, Benjamin!'

'Neither was I, Joel. That's not how I heard the prison guards accompany prisoners.' Benjamin rose to his feet and dusted off his clothes, still massaging his chin with one hand. 'Good job, kid. You saved us. And yourself.'

Saul stood frozen on the deck, his eyes on the guards lying in their blood. The other 'tourist' took the guns and other valuables from the guards' pockets. Benjamin and Joel picked up the short guard's corpse and threw it over the edge of the deck, followed by his colleague's. Saul watched over the cliff as the lifeless bodies flailed on their way down and turned into dots that disappeared in the waters below.

'It's almost seven. People will start coming over. We need to go.' Benjamin waved at Saul to follow him to the car.

'I need to go home. I need to see my mother.'

***

'They'll come searching for the guards in a couple of hours, ' Kat, the female assailant, said while driving the car to drop off Saul at home.

'We're lucky, I think it will rain. It should wash off the earth.' Benjamin moaned, still massaging his chin. 'Don't worry, kid. She must be fine.' He then patted Saul on the shoulder. 'You saved all of us.'

Saul didn't open his mouth for fear of either screaming or vomiting before passing out. The drizzle on the windshield turned into a strong summer rain as they passed through the familiar streets leading to Saul's house. He prepared for the worst and best. Images that he couldn't escape flashed before his eyes. As soon as their car came to a halt before a red light at the last intersection leading to the street where Saul had lived, he opened the car door and sprinted the longest five hundred meters of his life. His throat burned; his tears mixed with the pouring rain.

Saul stopped in front of an empty house that used to be his home. No curtains, no furniture, nothing to conceal, nothing to reveal.

'Where are you? Where are you?' He dropped to his knees on the doorstep and punched the wooden frame. The window of the next-door neighbor opened, and a curvy woman with a baby at her bosom appeared.

'She's gone. She died two days ago, stuck her head in the oven. They emptied the house yesterday,' the new mother, who didn't recognize Saul, said to the grieving boy. 'Did you know the family?'

A hand gripped Saul's shoulder, and Benjamin pulled him to his feet.

'Sorry to bother you, lady.' Benjamin gestured towards the neighbor, who was squinting to recognize the people on the porch. 'We were their extended family, but I guess we're too late now.' He then dragged Saul back to the car.

'Yes. You should have been here yesterday for the furniture. Now the municipality will be auctioning it off.'

'Pity. Have a nice day.'

The trio got into the car, and Kat slammed on the gas pedal, taking them away from the streets drenched under the downpour.

'Let me go! Let me go! It's all my fault, Mother. Forgive me!' Saul yelled, blabbered, cursed, and punched his head in the car. His organs, replaced by burning coals, were setting his insides on fire and choking his throat. 'You didn't deserve this. I did. Take me back to the cliff, Benjamin. I beg you. It should have been me.'

Benjamin took Saul's head in his palms and turned his face. 'It wasn't her or you that caused this. We're going to take our revenge on the ones who did this to you, to her, and everyone we loved. I promise.' bound in pain, the pair hugged.

Saul and the trio, who were now commiserating with the boy, cried in the car on their way outside the city. They shed tears for Daisy, Saul, the loved ones they had lost, and the loved ones they would lose, as life and love are ephemeral. Eventually, lovers pay the price of love in full through separation, either by will or misfortune, sometimes suddenly, more often gradually.

That was the last time Saul ever cried.

Part 6

A mixture of manure, ammonia, and hay found its way through his nostrils to his lungs. To give time for his olfactory receptors to get adjusted to the smell and gradually grow numb to the odor, Saul thought about breathing through his mouth at the entrance to the barn. But decided against it as the potential of tasting the air proved more repulsive. However, in the month he was here, Saul was getting used to the farm day by day, to the acrid smells, incessant bellowing of the animals, and the grueling work. He even appreciated how exhausting the work was, as it turned out to be easier to fall asleep at night. Besides, to be fair to the animals, he surely wasn't emanating a lilac scent either while running from barn to barn under the scorching sun and being drenched with sweat because of the high humidity. 'It must be better during the winter,' he thought and wiped away sweat from his brow.

Another farm worker grunted a greeting and passed by him to shovel out the manure. He was one of the two dozen fugitives from the city who, along with their families, had found a new life on Benjamin's farm. Similar to Saul, what gathered them all here was not their love of the countryside but the necessity of the circumstances that made them seek shelter from the city. Nowadays, the small society, created by word of mouth, only discussed two things: complaints about milk prices and hatred for the upcoming referendum.

Saul entered the lamb enclosure, next to the freshly sheared ewes, to pick up one of them to slaughter for the BBQ over the weekend. As he walked among the lambs, he could not help but feel like a deity deciding upon the fate of its subjects. He grinned to himself, thinking about the optics of what he was doing, and remembered Joel's words: 'The trick is not to name them. Before the slaughter, at least.' He then decided upon the one closest to himself, a white nine-month-old lamb, and haltered it with great struggle. He had to be extra careful, as haltering the animal with the long knife attached to his stump created the risk of poking himself or the lamb in the eye.

He led the rather docile animal to behind the barn, tipped it over the grass, and restrained it with his left leg. To expose the bare throat, he pulled the halter back with his right hand and made a deep cut that nearly simultaneously severed the trachea, carotid artery, and jugular veins with the long knife that took the place of his long-gone arm.

Saul rose to his feet as the lamb kicked its legs and convulsed. But Saul knew the animal felt nothing. Joel taught him why the animal shook while dying: 'When you sever the trachea and arteries, you are cutting the oxygen supply to the brain, which dies shortly after. Instead, the spinal cord takes control of the body. The clonic seizures after the cut don't mean the animal is suffering. A living being does not exist anymore.'

Now Saul had to wait a couple of minutes until the still-beating heart pumped out the blood. Then, he could skin, cut, clean, and hang the carcass, which needed to rest for three days in the fridge. Grueling work. Especially with a single arm. But now, with the help of the strapped-on knife, it was manageable alone.

He sat on the grass and watched the blood flow out as the lamb stopped jerking. He closed his eyes, and a nightmare flooded his consciousness; a still imagery of his mother sitting next to him on the bed, talking about vampires. *'Will I ever be able to re-live those moments without a gut-wrenching guilt?'* he wondered.

As soon as they arrived at the farm, Saul jumped on Benjamin to learn why the latter did not disclose the details of the escape so Saul could have let his mother know. While Joel and Kat peeled the pair apart, Benjamin shook his head and wiped away his own tears. 'I didn't know they were going to tell your mother, Saul. Trust me. I had not trusted you enough to tell you all the details, but I would have done so if I knew the guards were going to call your mother. I'm sorry.' Saul slipped away from Joel's grip and took a step towards Benjamin to punch him in the face. But upon seeing Benjamin, tears still rolling down his cheek, not flinching, Saul sprinted away to the woods surrounding the farm, only to return by dusk.

Guilt filled every second of his consciousness if his body was not performing a mind-numbing repetitive task. He thought of Sophie once more. 'Why am I still thinking about you?' Saul groaned. 'Get out of my head.' He punched the ground, frightening a nearby grasshopper.

***

'Of course, you can't move the fingers, but at least it will stop people outside the farm from gawking,' Kat said and slid the silicone prosthetic arm over the knife. Saul looked at the hand that was slightly bigger than the original one. Kat had tried to mirror Saul's right hand to create a prosthetic for the left but failed. So, she modeled it after Benjamin's left hand.

'Now you can go to the city for a stroll,' Joel said and patted Saul on the back.

'Kat did a great job with that hand. It even has hairs and veins,' Benjamin said as he joined the trio. He was holding his hands, which were covered by manure, in front of his body.

'I'm sure there's some other way to treat germaphobia,' Kat said as she held her nose.

'Go change your clothes,' Benjamin told Saul, threatening to touch Joel's face, who stepped back in disgust.

'But I was going to clean the stable.'

'Kat can do that, no worries. We need to meet someone important in the city.' Kat didn't seem excited about the new task but limited her objection to only spitting on the ground.

***

After finding a suitable spot for their car near the entrance of the park, Saul and Benjamin sat down on the closest bench. The gigantic park, surrounded by highways from all sides, was empty except for sparsely planted lonely trees and accompanying benches underneath them. On this Monday at noon, there was no one else in the park besides them to enjoy the highway view and the apartments towering beyond.

'Do you know why there's an armrest on the benches all around the city?' Benjamin said and tapped on the metal bar.

'I don't know. Is it more comfortable?' Saul asked, leaning back and putting his elbows on the bar separating him from his companion.

'No. Absolutely not.' Benjamin chuckled. 'Designers did not have your comfort in their mind. Bars are there so homeless people can't sleep on them.'

'Hmm.' Saul furrowed his brow to think about the last time he saw someone sleeping on the streets. 'I've never seen a homeless person before.'

'We don't let them survive here. That's why.'

Two police officers on motorcycles pulled behind their car and started inspecting the trunk. Then, the tall one with a thin beard pointed out the pair sitting on the bench to his colleague, a stocky woman. Saul stiffened up and straightened his posture as the cops walked towards them.

'Are you lost, officers?' Benjamin asked before the cops could say anything.

'Why would we be?' the mustachioed officer replied but was cut off by his partner. 'Is this your car, gentlemen?'

'Do you need a ride, officers?'

'Your taillight is broken. I need to write you a ticket,' the mustachioed officer, annoyed by what he saw as Benjamin's insolence, said and pulled a pad from his pocket. 'Please fix it as soon as possible.' As her partner scribbled the fine, the other cop's eyes wandered a second longer than usual over Saul's silicone hand, who, upon noticing the gaze, crossed his arms to hide the lifeless limb.

Benjamin nodded back to the officers, folded and put the ticket in his wallet. 'Ride safe, officers!' He then turned back to Saul. 'What was I saying? Oh, the benches. The municipality plans everything: how many people will sit together, where they will sit, and when they can sit based on the sun and the weather.'

'You seem to know a lot.'

'I do. I used to be an architect for urban planning on the city council,' Benjamin said and noticed Saul still looking behind the police officers. 'Do not worry about them,' Benjamin pointed to the cops getting on their motorcycles. 'A friend of mine in the municipality said we're registered as dead.' He then laid back and waved at the police officers leaving. 'How convenient it can be,' he grinned, 'to be dead?'

'Benjamin. You asked me to keep waiting. What is our plan to stop the change to the constitution?' Saul said and leaned forward to look into Benjamin's eyes. 'We have a month left, but all you're doing is brooding by yourself and chasing the cows around. We're on your side. What's the plan?'

'City planning was fine. I loved the job,' Benjamin continued, ignoring Saul's question. 'You decide where rich people live, where poor people may travel by public transport. Even where people can gather to protest or how much sunlight we're going to allow each neighborhood to see from the skyscrapers. How tall should the railings be on a bridge? Never higher than the waistline, by the way.'

'Playing God definitely stroked your ego the right way,' Saul puffed and tried to control the anger teeming in his throat.

'Have you seen the first cities ever built ten thousand years ago?' Benjamin ignored Saul one more time. 'There were no streets, and all the houses were cobbled together, and people entered from the roof.' He then turned and waved to a guy walking towards them. 'I always wondered what happened to those who couldn't climb the stairs.'

***

'Dana.'

'Saul. Nice to meet you.'

'Likewise, young man.'

Dana, an effeminate man in his late forties, sat next to Benjamin, crossed his legs and lit a cigarette. Saul thought that in contrast to Benjamin, who was a handsome man, Dana, with his clean-shaven face, plucked eyebrows, and well-fitting striped navy suit, was instead a beautiful human with warm brown eyes.

'They say cigarettes kill,' Benjamin said and waved a cloud of smoke away from his face. 'That it's bad for your lungs.'

'Huh. That cologne of yours is worse for my lungs…' Dana took a deep breath from his cigarette and blew on Benjamin's face. '… and for my heart. But cigarettes at least give me some pleasure first.' Upon seeing Benjamin's irritation, Saul felt a guilty pleasure that someone had finally managed to get under Benjamin's skin.

'You could have visited us on the farm.'

'Not fond of poultry.'

'We only have cattle and…'

'All the same to me.' Dana interrupted Benjamin, fluttered his eyelashes, and ended the conversation with a gentle wave. 'I don't like this park, Saul. It makes me feel small and irrelevant with its vast emptiness. The park shows how much we are constrained in space and also in time.'

'That's why some people find meaning in a religion or cult that promises them a goal beyond their fleeting existence,' Benjamin replied without waiting for Saul's comment. 'Is that why you joined the temple, Dana?' Now, it was Dana's turn to ignore Benjamin.

'Have you ever visited the temple, Saul?'

'I have not.'

'You should. Magnificent architecture with an impressive collection of art inside, depicting nymphs taking part in stories of a long-gone religion.' He again inhaled deeply but blew the smoke away this time to not tempt Benjamin further. 'There is also an aging man in charge of the temple, a skilled orator. I heard he's afflicted by an illness. He will… how to say it?' he then took another breath from the cigarette '… quit the post soon. You should definitely see him before that.'

***

Before they got back to the car, Saul stopped Benjamin.

'Do we have some time before we go back? I need to do something. Alone.'

'I have to visit another friend as well. I would have wanted you to come, but I can handle it by myself,' Benjamin said a moment after studying Saul's face. 'Then, let's meet in front of the municipality building in two hours. Okay?'

'Yes. See you there.'

As Saul turned his back, Benjamin caught him by the stump and turned him around. 'I'll explain everything once we get to the farm. I trust you.' Saul's eyes lingered over Benjamin's face, which shone with nothing but sincerity. 'I'm truly sorry about your mother. And everyone else you've lost. I am. We will avenge them and the others.'

***

Saul had been there only once, nearly a year ago, but he was sure of finding his way again. The pain had etched all the directions deep inside him. All the steps, turns, and the silence that tortured him since.

***

After Saul had pulled Sophie away from the cliff, they picked up her guitar and headed back to the bus, where their friends who had witnessed the entire debacle were waiting for them. As Sophie drunkenly shambled in Saul's arms, Ezra jumped out of the bus to walk back with them and picked up her guitar from Saul.

The bus greeted them with a solid silence, which evaporated once the engine roared and the wheels pounded on the road again. Saul threw himself next to Poppy as Ezra and Sophie sat in a muted vacuum in front of them. While Poppy rambled on about the birds they'd spotted, Saul sufficed with an occasional hand squeeze and a gentle nod to keep her speaking while focusing on the silence emanating from the seat in front.

Despite Poppy's taciturn opposition and confusion as to why her boyfriend was getting involved in a matter that was not his business, once the bus dropped them in the city center, Saul insisted on walking Sophie back home with Ezra. As the trio meandered along the streets towards Sophie's home, they kept their vows of silence intact. On the last stretch, the girl who should have been lost in the diamond froth on her way to the sea instead drowned her companions in her tears as they choked up, searching for words of consolation. Only Ezra mustered enough will to mutter, 'Don't cry, Sophie. Don't,' and put one arm around her slender shoulders, which were quietly bobbing up and down.

The stupefied pair watched as the girl climbed the stairs of her porch. She turned around one last time to look at them to express her gratitude mixed with shame.

'I'm sorry. I didn't mean to bother you.'

A meager stream of 'no problem,' 'take care,' and 'good evening' flowed out of them, assuaging their consciences by granting her the sought-after pardon.

***

Out of the corner of his eye, Saul noticed a guy in a brown suit who took the last three turns along with him while maintaining a rigid distance between them. To confirm his suspicion of being followed, Saul rotated counter-clockwise around a block while keeping an eye on the potential stalker through the shop windows they passed by.

Once he ended up back at the starting point with the guy still on his tail, Saul turned into an alleyway. He took cover against the wall and put his right hand on the prosthetic arm, ready to unsheathe the long knife. His heart started pounding faster as the footsteps got closer, step by step, beat by beat.

As he prepared to tackle the guy before the stalker turned the corner, Saul saw a stroller appear. Before Saul could pull himself back, the mother behind the stroller jumped in the air.

'You scared me, young man!'

'I'm sorry, ma'am. I was just... I was just waiting for my friend. And I was looking for shade. I am sorry.'

After the mother and stroller passed by, Saul got back on the street, but the man in the brown suit had disappeared.

***

Saul climbed the stairs leading up to the porch where Sophie once stood. He was planning to tell her family the same story he had told Sophie's boyfriend. 'I'm here for a research project. Why did your daughter kill herself? Any note that she had left?'

'No one's home,' the girl sitting on the porch said in a melodious voice. Saul stepped back as the girl walked towards him. She was a petite, curvy girl in her late teens with silky short black hair that fell in front of her peeping brown eyes. She wore bright indigo jeans and a plaid shirt with rolled-up sleeves. Saul couldn't help but think she looked like a fox. A pretty she-fox.

'I'll stop by later, then.'

'They'll probably come soon. You can wait with me if you want. Or maybe I can help. Faye.'

'Ben' Saul introduced himself but cursed at his lack of creativity to pick another name. 'Is Sophie's family still living here?'

'They are. Do you have time? Come sit with me.' Faye pointed back to her porch. 'I was a friend of Sophie's. I know the family.' He walked over to the girl's porch. When Faye turned her back, he put his prosthetic hand in his pocket, which would have caught her attention otherwise.

Saul squeezed next to Faye on the stairs of her porch as her flowery perfume dizzied his head. 'I was knitting a teddy bear.' She held up an almost finished blue bear with red buttons as eyes that dangled down from her needles. 'You must think it's very lame and girly.' She then blushed and pulled the teddy bear back onto her lap.

'Yes. I mean no,' Saul stuttered. 'I mean, it *is* girly but not lame. Not girly in a bad way. I mean, it's really cute.' Saul stumbled his way toward a coherent sentence.

'You think so?' Faye beamed and held up the teddy bear again.

'I do.' Saul said, now blushing himself, and inhaled deeply to taste her flowery scent once more, a guilty pleasure that caused him to blush even faster. He thought he wouldn't feel so uncomfortable if Faye broke eye contact once in a while. There was a natural ratio of looking into someone's eyes and then away, which seemed unknown to Faye. As she stared deep into him, his eyes dropped to her slim neck, then were drawn back to two brown magnets.

'What do you want from them?' Faye nodded towards Sophie's house.

'I'm... doing a research project for college,' Saul said and tried to move further away from her but only managed to get a breath away as his back hit the railings. 'I was going to ask them why Sophie killed herself.'

'Grim research. But I guess someone needs to do it for us,' Faye said and began knitting the bear's paws. The clicking of the needles fused into her melodious voice, making it harder for Saul to concentrate. 'She wasn't close to her parents. I don't think they would know much. Her father drove her to the park. I was in the window upstairs. She waved goodbye to me.' She then lifted her head once again and drilled her eyes into Saul. 'Did you love her?'

'Me? No! I think you misunderstood. I didn't know her. It's just for research,' Saul stammered, trying to escape her gaze, and pressed his back harder to the railings. He took a deep breath and smelled her perfume again. He regained his composure, listening to the rhythmic clicking of the needles dancing in her little dexterous fingers, and pressed on after a minute. 'But I guess you were close. Do you know why she committed suicide?'

'Do you go to school?'

'I do. Why? I told you I was doing a research project for the university,' Saul said in a higher pitch than he would have liked. Faye didn't react to him and kept on knitting.

'You know what they teach us in school?' she said and pretended to mimic a monotonous robotic voice: 'The reason people kill themselves is usually a manifestation of an underlying disturbance through the weakest point in their psyche.' She then lifted the bear to show Saul, who nodded to approve of her skills. 'Don't you believe that?'

'I don't know. Do you know what bothered her?'

'She was always moody but became worse after dating a new guy. She kind of felt guilty for cheating on her then-boyfriend. Girly stuff. Boys would never feel guilty. Do you have a girlfriend, Ben?'

'I don't.'

'Me neither.'

'What?'

'Never mind.'

'Time, I left,' Saul, who could not cope with the stress anymore, said and jumped back to his feet. 'Thank you for your time. By the way, do you know, perchance, the name of the new guy?'

'I do.' Faye lowered her eyes back to the teddy bear. 'Ezra. The guy who you brought Sophie back with.'

***

Benjamin pulled near the entrance of the park housing the Farewell Tree.

'I won't go there,' Saul said and shook his head.

'Shame. I always liked to take a stroll here before. I'm not planning to go in, either. I'm waiting for an acquaintance,' Benjamin said and rolled down the window on his side. 'You know the story of the Farewell Tree, right? Tell me.'

'I do,' Saul replied and summarized what he had read in Mrs. Pallas's room. A memory that now seemed eons ago.

'Huh. Utter propaganda. Distortion,' Benjamin said and snorted with ridicule. 'After the vassal kidnapped the blacksmith's wife. The latter tried to sneak into the castle of the vassal but ran into guards and ended up killing one of them. But the blacksmith had to run away.' Benjamin retold his account as, across the empty street, another car parked near the entrance. 'The vassal sent a letter to the blacksmith's family saying that if the young man didn't turn himself in, the vassal was going to torture the woman.'

Three women in their late thirties, probably related to each other, stepped out of the car and walked to the arch. Benjamin stopped his story and watched them walk across. 'The blacksmith ended up turning himself in, and as a punishment, the vassal made him design the steel noose and hang himself as if he'd committed suicide,' Benjamin continued, rolled his window up, and started the engine. 'If those maggot villagers had done something, the blacksmith would have killed the vassal. No, he did not kill himself. The vassal did not kill the blacksmith. The villagers' docility killed him.' One of the women hugged the others and walked into the park alone. Benjamin's knuckles had turned white from squeezing the steering wheel.

'Do you know the woman walking in?' Saul asked as they hit the road once again.

'I do.' Benjamin replied. 'She's my little sister.'

***

In the falling twilight, the pair sat in silence on their way back to the farm. Saul re-lived every moment he was with Faye, while Benjamin kept a stone face and sighed occasionally. Once they arrived at their destination, Saul was the first to break the silence:

'I'm sorry about your sister.'

'Our plan is to kill the people who are planning to commit suicide. If we just stop them, they will eventually try again because committing suicide is a way for them to take control. We're going to start tomorrow in the temple. The man in charge of the temple, let's call him a priest, is a very influential man. Tomorrow night, after his sermon, we are going to ask him to renounce his plans to kill himself and support us in the referendum.' Benjamin said, keeping his eyes on the steering wheel. Saul turned to his companion but could read nothing from him as Benjamin's face was in shadow.

'What if he doesn't listen?'

'We'll improvise.'

'Do people usually listen?'

'No. Never. There are romantics out there. I used to be one of them. I thought, if only you can show people how wrong they are, we'll fix everything. The problem is they know exactly what they're doing. Look at yourself, how brutally they came after you. I tried Saul. I tried talking to them. Let me tell you a story.'

***

Benjamin, no grays yet in his curly hair, walked into the courtroom and took his seat. Shortly after, the judge, a comely woman in her fifties with two French braids around her head, took her seat on the bench. Benjamin couldn't take his eyes off the shining square-shaped diamond on her finger and the accompanying pearls on her bosom. Under her long eyelashes, two azure eyes stroked across the room as she bared her tiny teeth:

'The court will deliberate for the case from the plaintiff, Mr. Benjamin, against the city. Before the session is adjourned, the clerk will summarize the arguments. Any objections?' the judge then scanned the room momentarily. ' I see none. Please continue.'

'The plaintiff has asked the city immediately to build ramps in pavements and replace cobblestones with flat concrete slabs. Also, the entrances to public buildings should be wheelchair accessible, and funds made available for the accessibility-oriented renovation of private buildings. Additionally, the municipality must mandate new construction projects to be wheelchair accessible on the grounds that not doing so would mean the city violates Section 5.2.1 of the constitution to serve all citizens equally.'

'Any objections?'

'None, your honor,' Benjamin replied, wriggling in his chair and hunching forward.

'The city has argued against the case brought forward on three fronts. First, there is no need for the adjustments as currently pavements are not being used by wheelchairs, anyway.'

'What kind of backward logic is that?' Benjamin shouted and jumped up from his chair. 'They can't use it because it is not accessible, and you are arguing that there's no need because they are not going outside, anyway.' Benjamin pointed his finger toward the city's lawyers and slammed his fist on the table.

'Order!' The judge slammed the gavel. 'Order. This is your final warning, Mr. Benjamin,' she said, waving the gavel towards the plaintiff. 'Disturb the session once more, and we will continue without you present.' Benjamin huffed and puffed but slammed back in his chair and kept quiet.

'Secondly,' the clerk continued, 'as the clear and overwhelming majority of taxpayers would not use the ramps and other wheelchair accessibility improvements in the buildings, it would violate the public trust and funds delineated in Section 5.2.1 of the constitution to serve all citizens equally. Last but not least, the historic cobblestone pavements are not only part of the city's cultural heritage but an important part of the drainage solution that feeds underground water sources. Thus, their removal would have detrimental environmental and cultural consequences.'

'Any objections?' the judge said and glared down at Benjamin, who opened his mouth but closed it again as good sense prevailed. 'Session is adjourned for a break and deliberation before the final verdict.'

Benjamin looked at his hands, which seemed abnormally small and shapeless to him now. All the curves, knuckles, and hairs were foreign. As the court re-convened for the final verdict, he was trying to find his way back out of the maze of creases in his palms.

'All rise,' the clerk announced as the judge took her seat.

'The court has decided that the city is not guilty of violating the constitution as they acted in the best interests of taxpayers. As the proposed amenities would not be used by most citizens, they can be classified as luxurious and at times harmful to the cultural and environmental landscape of the city.'

'But may I not build them myself, out of my pocket, if the cost is the only issue?' Benjamin interrupted the judge and collapsed back in his chair.

'We warned you not to interrupt us, sir. I will give you one more chance,' the judge scolded Benjamin and pierced him with her shiny ice eyes. 'As ruled by the lower courts, the city declines that offer. Unauthorized construction poses safety risks to the public, and we will hand down a fine for damaging public property.'

'You are really haughty, judge, along with these idiots over there,' Benjamin said, pointing towards the city lawyers. He had prepared himself to raise hell, flip tables, and scream if he lost the case, but now, he was calm. A disturbing serenity stemming not from a place of comfort but from resignation took over him. 'You're all pretending you'll not be the ones in the wheelchair. Let me guess. You would just kill yourselves instead.'

'I understand your frustration, Mr. Benjamin. That is why I am being extra lenient with you,' the judge replied and fluttered her long eyelashes. 'But we all, as public servants and even as citizens, are doing our best for the society. We are only following the rule of law, and that is the source of our power.'

'No. No.' Benjamin laughed. 'Your source of power is the two meatheads standing in each corner of the room.' He pointed to two guards by the walls of the court. 'and your belief that I can't get to you before them.'

'How dare you ...' the court clerk tried to interrupt Benjamin.

'The one on the left is limping, slightly shifting his weight to his right leg and holding on to the railings to find his balance. Probably injured his calf,' Benjamin said as the courtroom fell into a trance of tension radiating from the plaintiff. 'One on the right has eye bags and didn't sleep all night. His wedding ring is still shiny, so that tells me he is a newlywed and a new father.' Benjamin took a deep breath and then sniffed the air a couple of times. 'I smell a five-month-old baby.' Another sniff. 'A baby girl. What's her name, Officer?' Benjamin asked and turned his eyes back to the judge, who was unfazed, sitting on the seat with a bored expression on her face. 'Despite your beliefs, I can get to you in two seconds, and they can only react in four. That would leave us two seconds.' Benjamin crossed his arms on his chest and slumped back. 'And I only need one second.'

'If your theatrics are over, I find you in criminal contempt of court and sentence you to one month in jail.' The judge finished gathering papers on her table and handed them over to the clerk. She stroked her pearls on her bosom. 'I'm in a good mood today, and I can suspend your sentence for a year if you apologize to the court now. Given you that you want to go home today.'

***

Twilight yielded to dusk, so stars and far-away galaxies appeared one after another in the night sky. They sat in the car and stared at the glimmering lights of the farmhouses, listening to crickets overtaking the night among the flashing fireflies. It was one of those hotter summer nights that made a person uncomfortable in his skin and impossible to sleep peacefully.

'Don't dwell on instances, Saul.' Benjamin interrupted the crickets. 'I blamed the instances before. But certain things are inevitable. If you hadn't pulled that girl away from the cliff, you were going to hold up one of your coworkers trying to hang themselves. I see that in you.' Saul stepped out of the car, but Benjamin stayed behind the wheel.

'Aren't you coming?'

'I'll sit a bit more.'

'Okay. Good night.'

As Saul stepped away, Benjamin leaned out of the window and shouted behind him.

'Saul!'

'What?'

'Thank you'

As Saul walked away, Benjamin put his forehead on the steering wheel and sailed away to the past. He was trying to escape for a long time.

***

'What happened, love?'

'I lost the case. I'm sorry. Forgive me.'

'That's okay, Ben. There's nothing to forgive. I know you did your best. Besides, you'll always be by my side to help.'

'I will. Always.'

***

After incessantly rolling around in his bed for what seemed like an eternity, Saul walked outside the house to throw himself into the hammock hanging between two oak trees. He didn't get to tire himself to sleep today, so it was going to be a sleepless night marred by nightmares for him. Besides, even if he wanted to sleep in the hammock now, the occasional buzzing of the mosquitos alerted him to remain vigilant lest he should wake up covered in itchy bites. Stars flashed behind the rustling leaves, revealing the fragmentations of a shattered cosmos in motion. Saul sailed among the stars from one corner of the universe to another in search of respite.

His soul was trapped in a shapeless pebble along the shore, dancing to the rhythm of the tide. As the waves rose, his chest swelled with an encompassing hatred of Ezra for what he had concealed, with the images of him sitting across the bench in the park, counting the minutes until Sophie's arrival, flaring in Saul's eyes. Once the waters ebbed, Saul's animosity receded, leaving behind a trail of confusion mixed with pity. Partly for himself, partly for Ezra.

Increasingly, he saw Benjamin as his only hope. He had imagined running away, living in the wilderness. But he felt it a duty to stop this inhumane plague here, right now, from contaminating the world any further. Then Mr. Lewis's words rang in his ears. 'As Aristotle said, only gods and monsters live alone.' Saul lifted his left arm and found himself akin to the latter.

***

Saul pulled the car in front of Faye's house and ran up the stairs of the porch. He knocked on the door twice, but no one answered. He knocked once more but heard no one. He pushed the handle down and opened the door. Guided by his senses, he ran upstairs to a room whose door was invitingly left ajar. As he approached the room, he heard the soothing metallic clicking sound. He pushed the door open and saw Faye sitting on the bed. She lifted the teddy bear in the air, and Saul approved once again, nodding to her skill. Without rushing, he approached the bed and dropped beside Faye's knees. Her fingertips ran through his hair and untied a knot deep inside him. Saul withdrew from her and lifted his prosthetic arm. While he took off the fake arm, he searched Faye's eyes for disgust and horror but found none. She then reached over and unstrapped the long knife, still dripping blood, from Saul's elbow. Now, in her warm eyes, he sought refuge and forgiveness, of which he found plenty. Saul sat next to her on the bed and pressed his face against hers. Once he withdrew, he was holding Sophie's hands.

***

Just at dawn, Saul woke up shaken from the dream, bitten all over his face and arms by mosquitoes overnight. Dreams were much worse than nightmares, as the former showed how his life was in tatters, and there was no waking up from it. He thought that Mrs. Pallas was right and no girl would ever want a crippled man like him. Even if Saul and Benjamin were successful and ultimately prevailed in the referendum to eventually roll back everything, what would it mean to him? Saul imagined himself slaughtering sheep and shoveling cow dung for the rest of his life.

He wanted to end it all. He wanted to see his mother again. Now, how much he wished for the afterlife depicted in the old religions to exist. But remembered, all of them condemned the people who killed themselves to eternal torture in hell. The only option then would be to wish for hell and heaven not to exist and to face the fact that he would never see his mother again. He closed his eyes to picture Daisy one more time in his room, talking about vampires. Pointing to the mirror and giggling. But he couldn't remember her face and panicked as if his mother was dying one more time inside him. The harder he searched, the harder he tried to paint a portrait, the more elusive she became. He wanted to end it all.

Saul's thoughts wandered off to the city and its inhabitants. Out there in the city, there must be a little boy or girl as desperate as he once was. If he didn't find the strength in his heart to fight for himself, he needed to find the courage to save them from the agony of prematurely losing their loved ones. Yet he knew all the losses were premature. Saul decided that rather than be forced to his knees because he couldn't fight his own problems, he wanted to get crushed under the boulder of a bigger cause for others.

***

'Uncle Delbert, Saul and I need to leave soon to go to the city.' Benjamin said.

'Alright, alright. Don't worry. We'll be back on time,' Uncle Delbert replied and winked at Saul walking beside him. 'I just once ran late to the restroom, and now there is no escape from him.' Uncle Delbert was most likely the oldest person Saul had ever seen. Despite his wrinkled skin, balding gray hair, and the need to lean on his cane as they climbed the small birch corpse, he was by no means a frail old man. He was a sturdy guy, just with wrinkles, balding white hair, and a wooden cane. Saul always likened him to an old sailor toughened by the sea.

'Don't we need a suit to handle bees?' Saul asked.

'Our hives are very docile. Some hives are harder to handle. For those, you indeed need a suit,' Uncle Delbert replied and pulled a handkerchief to wipe away sweat from his forehead. Saul noticed that inside both of his wrists, Uncle Delbert had a tattoo: 'DNR.' *Maybe it's the name of his wife,* Saul thought.

'How do I tell the difference between a docile and aggressive hive?'

'By how many times they are stinging you.' Uncle Delbert laughed and wheezed as they climbed the hill. 'I used to be a marriage celebrant. Once, I officiated a wedding covered in bee stings, which it turns out I was allergic to. Hah! You should have seen me. My lips and eyelids were all swollen.' Talking made Uncle Delbert run out of breath while climbing the hill, and he started panting heavily.

'Should we rest a bit?' Saul said

'No. No. We're almost there.'

They reached the top of the hill, covered in dandelions, where there were ten beehives in grey wooden boxes. 'Ah! Bloody Hell!' Uncle Delbert yelled and pointed towards one hive lying broken on the ground.

'What do you think happened? Can it be dogs?'

'Dogs don't do that. It can only be a honey badger. Pesky animals. I'll talk to Benjamin. We need a sturdy fence to keep them out. They'll surely come back otherwise.' As they approached the hives, the noise of the bees hit them like a wave and silenced even their internal thoughts.

Saul, at first, was nervous and tried to keep his distance from the hives, but as the bees buzzed around him without stinging him, he gained more confidence to get closer and help Uncle Delbert remove the debris left behind by the honey badger.

'Damn, animal probably ate nearly the entire colony. The queen must be dead, so leftover workers joined the other hives,' Uncle Delbert said, raising his voice to break through the buzzing and lifting a broken comb to show Saul. 'I'm pretty sure the bees put up a brave fight. Remarkable creatures. Did you know that if a parasite infects a worker bee, she flies off and kills herself instead of infecting the rest of the colony? Remarkable, indeed.' Uncle Delbert and Saul started smoking the hives so they could open up the lid and begin collecting honey.

'Did you meet your wife at a wedding? Mrs. DNR?'

'Ha!' Uncle Delbert laughed and chased a bee flying near his nose. 'I never got married. You know, unfortunately, the most beautiful girl in the wedding is usually taken.' He then unbuttoned his shirt to reveal the same three letters: 'DNR.'

'It means 'do not resuscitate.' I got them years ago. Don't get me wrong, I love living, but if I already dropped dead peacefully, let me leave peacefully.'

Saul smoked another hive and checked the combs. 'I'm not sure Benjamin would like that.'

'Ha! I'm almost twice his age. He can zip it.' Uncle Delbert pulled another comb and ran the uncapping knife along it. 'I think at times he is plain trying to get himself killed. Like the woman who killed a baby so she could get executed.'

'What? I've never heard of that,' Saul said and cursed under his breath as his hand got sticky from honey. It was extra tough to handle the combs one-handed. He jerked once a lone bee landed on his cheek, and he almost dropped the comb. 'Who killed the babies?'

'You see, in the old religions, committing suicide was the greatest sin. Because there was no way you could have asked forgiveness for it after you killed yourself. A direct ticket to hell.' He licked his finger. 'I like the pine honey more. But this is also nice. We have nice flora here.' Uncle Delbert then put the comb back in the hive and closed the lid. Saul felt he was getting a terrible headache from the constant buzzing. 'So, centuries ago, a religious lady found a loophole. If someone else killed her, she could go to heaven. Upon failing to find someone willing to kill her, she decided she needed to be executed instead. In her country at that time, only the people who killed children were executed.'

Uncle Delbert closed the lid of the hive after he finished checking the combs. He started breathing heavily as tending to bees under the heat of the noon sun began to get the better of him. So, he waved to Saul to take a small break under the birch trees. With Saul's help, he lowered himself to the grass and gave his back to the trunk. Now they could see the farm from the hill, the alfalfa and corn fields being worked by tractors behind the barns where Benjamin and a couple of others were trying to set up the new milking machines. In Saul's eyes, this meager farm of two dozen people was their only chance to reverse the fortunes of their city. He felt as if they were Atlas carrying the world not as a punishment but because they cared about the land where once his mother, sister, and Sophie had lived.

Among the grass peeked a daisy. He reflexively reached to pluck it but then let it be. He felt immense gratitude for doing the right thing, as if the world would have come tumbling down if he had uprooted the fragile flower. He knelt down to smell the daisy and took a deep breath. That was the day he learned daisies carried a mild scent reminiscent of cow dung. He sat back repulsed, feeling betrayed by the flower. He once again reached to pluck it out of revenge but let it be once again out of compassion.

'What happened then? Did she kill her own children?' Saul said, after a break, to give Uncle Delbert a chance to catch his breath after a coughing fit.

'No. No. She didn't have any.' Uncle Delbert continued his story. He coughed again and pulled out his handkerchief to wipe away sweat. 'She borrowed her neighbor's child and killed her. She then turned herself into authorities, confessed the crime, and repented for her sin so she could go to heaven.'

'Well, she was definitely stupid,' Saul laughed, but he saw that Uncle Delbert had grown serious.

'You never know how desperation can push someone down a path no one wants to go unless you feel truly desperate yourself.'

A loud boom interrupted their conversation as earth and dust flew into the air from a far corner of the farm. Once Saul reached the scene, Benjamin and Joel were sending away other people who had gathered around.

'Nothing to see. We were blasting a manure pit. It was louder than what we had expected.'

'At least give a warning beforehand next time!' one worker complained and cursed as she walked away. 'You scared the children!'

- 'I know. I know. I'm sorry,' Joel said and tried to hide a childish smile as he looked back to the new manure pit they'd created.

'Saul! You are finally here!' Benjamin broke off from the crowd and walked to him. 'Uncle finally set you free.'

***

Saul and Benjamin, dressed in nice suits, left for the temple in the evening. The former fought with Ezra in a thousand ways in his mind, while the latter voluntarily re-lived memories that would haunt someone forever. As they approached the temple, Saul broke the silence:

'How did you know the guard had a daughter?'

'What daughter?'

'The one in the court you told me about yesterday.'

'Ha!' Benjamin laughed. 'I'd heard them talking to each other in the court bathroom.'

The Freedom Philosophy followers had rebuilt most of the city from the ground up based on the architectural norms of an orderly society they dreamt of, apart from the city temple. People weaned off the old religions quickly; however, the temple stood as part of the routine of their lives for some who sought guidance and meditation to imbue the freedom philosophy deeper in their souls and minds— especially for those who, for some reason, had drifted away and could not feel happy for a former loved one who had released themselves from suffering by suicide. City officials believed that in two or three generations, the public would not need the clutches of the temple at all if the values, as the saying goes, would even be rooted in the hearts of the unborn.

Many times before, Saul had passed by the temple, which looked like a fairy tale palace with its intricate carvings, hideous gargoyles, and marble statues of saints of old religions who were promising their followers salvation. For the first time in his life, Saul stepped inside the temple. The interior was rather dimly lit and a lot cooler than Saul had expected. Two floors were filled with ancient statues and sculptures, which doubled as an art gallery for most of the week.

They sat near the exit on the right. On their side was a sculpture depicting a lustful man chasing a terrified woman who was transforming into a tree as her fingers became branches covered in marble leaves and her body turned into a marble trunk. Saul looked around and saw a couple of other sculptures of young women running away from men and other foul creatures.

Most of the people inside the temple had already taken their seats and were meditating with their eyes closed while waiting for the sermon to start. The others went around the long hall looking at the sculptures and colorful frescos. As he wriggled in his chair, Saul's hip pressed into something on Benjamin's side. He looked down and saw a gun tucked under Benjamin's shirt. They caught each other's eyes before Benjamin moved his suit to conceal the weapon before anyone else noticed it.

The door behind the podium opened, and an old man, visibly much younger than Uncle Delbert, emerged with an energetic gait to take center stage. Whatever Saul imagined him to be, the man was different. He wore a dark green blazer with gray jeans and sported a thick white handlebar mustache contrasting his balding head. His dark, energetic eyes complemented his aura of knowing authority. He lifted both his hands, which were trembling in a barely perceptible wavelength, and held them there as everyone else took their seats. Then he declared a moment of meditation:

'It must have been a long workday for most of us. Let's reflect on what lies behind us and what waits in front of us. Close your eyes.'

Saul hesitated to follow the instruction, but upon seeing Benjamin doing the same, he obliged with the request. Saul thought about how they were going to confront the orator while the latter forced himself to live through a painful memory that squeezed the air out of his lungs. But Benjamin had to remember why he had come to the temple.

***

Benjamin parked the car near the temple and went back to the trunk to pull out a wheelchair. He then opened the side door and helped his wife to shift to the wheelchair. She had a pure beauty that was worthy of the apple from Paris. Her elegant yet modest pastel-colored dress and tightly held ponytail stood in sharp contrast to her husband, who wore a dark grey suit with a loosened tie while sporting a week-old beard. Benjamin pushed the wheelchair over the curb until he reached the stairs of the temple entrance. He hissed and shook his head in frustration.

'I'll carry you inside, then I'll come back for the wheelchair.' He then picked up his wife. 'Wow, someone's putting on a lot of weight recently,' he huffed and puffed to pretend he was struggling to carry her.

'Shut up!' she pinched his chin.

'Ouch!' Benjamin tried to bite her fingers but was not fast enough. 'Remind me to declaw you when we get back home.'

'No, sir, please. I promise, I'll behave.' She then hid her hands under her armpits. But once Benjamin looked away, she pinched him again. She giggled and pressed her head to Benjamin's neck to feel his heartbeat and smell his bergamot cologne. He looked down at her pretty face and once again felt like the luckiest man on earth. He wanted to squeeze her into his chest so they could become one to live and die together. That had to happen. He did not want to die before her as it maddened him to think how she would survive alone. He did not want to die after her, as the world without her presence would be nothing but hell. So, he concluded they had to die together, holding hands, losing their minds in the depths of each other's eyes as their souls intertwined to form something bigger than them.

He pinched her bottom and made her squeal. 'Tit for tat. No mercy.'

After he helped her wife sit on a chair near the door, he went back to fetch the wheelchair. The couple wandered in the marble halls to admire the many artwork inside, then stopped in front of a giant sculpture that depicted a man and his two sons being strangled by an enormous snake. The sons on each side of the man were desperately looking at their father, who, in turn, had his pleading eyes on the sky for heavenly help from a *deus ex machina*.

'Do you think they got away, Ben?'

'They're not real.'

'You must be real fun at parties,' she said and tried to roll her wheelchair over Benjamin's foot, but he jumped to the side in time.

'It's an exquisite piece, is it not?' The white handlebar mustachioed man appeared next to them. 'Gregory,' he shook hands with the couple. 'I'm the curator of the temple.'

'The priest then,' Benjamin said with a visible contempt he did not try to hide. His wife pulled on Benjamin's suit jacket and whispered, 'Behave!'

'No, I'm not a priest; that is in the past. Our sermons are not about God or responsibilities. They are only reflections of us.' Gregory, concealing any frustrations he might have, explained without breaking eye contact with Benjamin, who opened his mouth to reply, but as his wife tugged his jacket again, he swallowed his answer and his ego.

'Nice to meet you. I am Marie, and this is my husband, Ben. Can you tell us more about this sculpture?'

'It stands out from the other sculptures and frescos of the ancient world as this depicts a pain without a reason, sacrifice or martyrdom.' He then pointed to the head of the snake biting the father's hip. 'Just a family against the forces of nature.'

The artist must have been very talented. The agony and desperation in their faces are real. I like to imagine that they managed to escape. I believe in happy endings,' she said and looked at her husband, who sufficed with rolling his eyes.

'I think escaping from pain is always possible. One way or another.' Gregory twirled his white mustache. 'I believe we are living in a multiverse with endless possibilities, and our consciousness is drifting from one to another. Then why stay in a place where we are in pain and at a disadvantage? Good day to you.' Gregory took a step and turned his back. Benjamin saw the light in Marie's face turn off.

'What if you're wrong, Gregory?' Benjamin asked with contempt, squeezing his wife's shoulder. 'What if there's no other universe, and this is our only reality?'

'Even so, I don't see any reason for someone to imprison themselves to suffering.' Gregory said and turned away from the couple. 'Enjoy the gallery.'

***

The short meditation ended after a single clap from Gregory:

'Let's start with an announcement. Today will be my last sermon.' A collective sigh rose from the audience, but after a single clap that started a domino effect, the mood shifted from initial shock to gratitude for the orator's service. Gregory hushed the room and put an end to the commotion. 'Health-wise, I am no longer in a position to fulfill my duties or independently live my life to the fullest. I am in a condition which will get exponentially worse.' He took another pause and walked to the other side of the stage. He had a natural charisma that captivated his audience's undivided attention. Saul felt sorry for the man and felt an uncomfortable tingling sensation in his missing arm. He then turned to Benjamin, who had the same expression as the tiger just before it pounced on Saul and was directed at Gregory.

'I led a happy life. The time will come for all of us to say farewell. I wish we could say it on our terms for all of us. I am planning to commit suicide in three days, on Friday.' Another pause from Gregory. 'Which gives us three days to say goodbye and sort out the succession for the curator of the temple.' He walked back to his starting position in a triangular route. 'Yet, we have another sermon to get through.'

***

'I want to end with one last story.' Gregory raised his trembling hands in the air again. Saul's muscles tensed up, and an icy shiver dashed through his veins. Benjamin shifted to the edge of his seat.

'We always cherish the victors. But those who lost are sometimes just as laudable. I guess everyone has heard of the great Roman statesman...' He took an unexpected pause and looked around the room with immense concentration but sighed and eventually pulled notes from his pocket. 'Julius Caesar.' After skimming the papers, he tried to put the crumpled papers back in his pocket, but deciding he might need them once more, he held the notes in his hand. 'But we should also know about Cato, a great Roman senator of the Republic.' Gregory then walked to the center of the stage. 'Cato was staunchly against corruption, nepotism, and cronyism. When...' He took another pause and made a grimace. Then he looked at his notes again and huffed, '... Julius Caesar won a decisive victory and cleared the last hurdles to transform the Republic into an empire and himself into an emperor; Cato stood by his ideals. Refusing to obey the rule of an emperor, in an act of defiance and for the honor of the Roman Republic, he stabbed himself with his own...' Resigning to his fate, after a brief moment, he looked up the word in his notes: 'sword.' Although dampened by the interruptions throughout the sermon, Gregory, in relief at finishing the final short story, found his voice again and managed to attract the attention of the audience once more, 'Tell me now. Was Cato a coward? Was he a selfish person? Was he wrong to defy a dictator?' He asked as his voice went up with each question while he wagged his index finger at the audience members. 'Do not fear taking your own destiny into your hands!' he shouted at the top of his lungs, which generated enthusiastic applause from the crowd. He scanned the long gallery to enjoy the effect of his speech and bowed his head before calling for another moment of reflection. That was the last sermon Gregory gave.

***

After the last people gathered below the podium shook hands and wished well for Gregory left, the curator went back in through the same door he entered. All along, Saul and Benjamin pretended to be looking at the sculptures.

'We're closing. You can come back tomorrow.'

Saul turned around and saw Dana, wearing the same well-fitting suit he wore in the park yesterday, but with a fresh shirt.

'We were hoping to meet privately with the curator. Would it be possible?' Benjamin said as Saul stood in silence in the palpable tension.

'Are you sure, Benjamin?' Dana said after a moment.

'I am.'

'I understand. Follow me.'

Dana led them through the gallery to a door that opened to a narrow corridor followed by a steep staircase.

'First room on the left.'

'Thank you.'

Dana opened his mouth to say something but changed his mind. He reached into his pocket and lit a cigarette.

'I'll be in the gallery.'

'I didn't know we could smoke here. It would have made the sermon bearable.' Benjamin said and asked Saul to walk up the stairs.

'If no one sees, no rule is broken.'

'Indeed. Indeed.'

Benjamin knocked on the carved door depicting a scene from an old religious text.

'Dana? Come in,' Gregory answered from the other side.

Benjamin, followed by Saul, entered the well-lit room, which only held three chairs, a black desk, and a wall full of books.

'Who are you? Did we have a meeting scheduled?' Gregory asked as he rose to his feet. Gregory contorted his face to something between surprise and confusion. Saul noticed the kind tone in the orator's voice indicating the suspicion that, indeed, they might have a meeting.

'We have come to talk with you, sir,' Benjamin said and sat in the chair across the orator. Waiting near the entrance, Saul hesitated for a moment, but Benjamin asked him to close the door and take a seat next to him.

'As you can see, gentleman, I'm busy. Did we have a meeting scheduled? If not, I will kindly…' Gregory said and pointed to the door.

'I am kindly asking you to take a seat,' Benjamin interrupted him. 'It won't take long, I promise.' After Gregory slumped in his chair, Benjamin rose from his and opened a window in the small room. 'It is boiling in here/ If you don't mind…'

'I do, gentleman. Please introduce yourself or leave my room at once.'

'May I ask you what illness afflicts you?' Benjamin returned to his chair.

'Why do you ask? Who are you?' Gregory said, and he gripped the edge of his table. Saul saw the unease growing in the orator and seeds of fear taking root in the old man's face. With each passing second, Gregory seemed increasingly more fragile. Saul worried the man would break his fingers merely by clenching the table.

He turned into Benjamin, who hid behind a mask of aloofness that was only betrayed by the seeping anger visible at the corners of his mouth and eyes.

'I'd guess Parkinson's. Based on the tremors in your hands, memory loss, and struggling to find the right words.'

'What do you want from me?' Gregory asked, gaining a little more composure.

Benjamin stood up and pointed to the letters Gregory was signing.

'Do you know what letters he is signing, Saul? He is signing encouragement letters to people who have an appointment with the Farewell Tree.' Benjamin slammed the table and sent a fountain pen up in the air, which then rolled to the floor. Saul looked at the letters, then to Gregory's face, which was now devoid of any perceptible emotion. Saul imagined Sophie in her room opening the letter, giving her courage, promising her the end of her troubles. 'How is it fair that I get judged for trying to rescue her while they condemn her to death without knowing her reasons?' He fumed as any trace of compassion for Gregory, who he saw as one of the culprits for the death of Sophie, disappeared. And Alice. And Daisy. And many others. Gregory's eyes caught the gun on Benjamin's hip, but the curator remained unfazed.

'I'll tell you what I want only once, so listen carefully.' Benjamin put his palms on the table and leaned forward to the curator. 'First, you will send letters asking people to reconsider their decision. Second, you will not kill yourself, at least publicly, to generate attention. I know you're trying to turn it into a spectacle.' Once Gregory learned what the intruders wanted from him, he seemed much more relaxed and took a comfortable position in his chair.

'What if I agree and then immediately call the police?' Gregory grinned.

'I don't know.' Benjamin scratched his chin. 'Maybe I'll call and ask your daughter Caroline for advice?'

'Do not get her involved!' Gregory roared and slammed his fist on the table.

'Those people you are sending letters to are someone else's daughters, mothers, and lovers. Idiot!' Benjamin screamed back. 'Why don't you think about those people?'

'Those people signed off on their free will. They...'

'Bullshit!' Benjamin interrupted him. 'You know they're forced as well as I do. Not with a gun to their head. But by cobblestones in the pavements, by shunning every single different kid in the school, by stigmatizing the fat, the old, and the poor. By presenting death as an antidote to the illness that is called life. By sending these stupid letters.' He grabbed one and tore to pieces it in front of Gregory.

'Do you know how my dementia and Parkinson's will end? Being unable to care for myself, forgetting my loved ones. Who are you to condemn me to that suffering?' asked Gregory.

'Eventually, there will be a cure.'

'Eventually, there will be other illnesses without cures.' Gregory shook his head. 'Can't you see that we have eradicated homelessness, hunger, and even unemployment?'

'Ha! You've already gone mad!' Benjamin laughed, turned to Saul, and pointed to Gregory. 'You've only eliminated the homeless, hungry, and unemployed.'

'I see you are in pain. Probably you've lost people you cared for,' Gregory said in a soft and understanding voice. 'I lost people too. Nothing will bring them back. I would have gladly sacrificed my life for them. But I can't condemn to suffering for my own happiness.' He leaned back in his chair and put his elbows on the arms. Benjamin pulled the gun from his hip and pointed it at Gregory. Saul rose to his feet. Part of him wanted to take the gun away from Benjamin and end the masquerade. Part of him wanted to take the prosthetic arm out and stab the old man. 'How can you do this to Sophie?' Instead, he froze and let fate play out.

'Will you do as I say?' Benjamin said and aimed at the man's head.

'I am planning to die in three days, anyway.' The orator laughed. 'Do you think I would feel...?' Gregory paused and squirmed as he searched for the right word.

'Did you want to say afraid?'

'You won't find peace even if you ...'

'Go to hell.'

***

Benjamin put the gun on the table and searched Gregory's desk and drawers. Before Benjamin got to the second drawer, Saul heard quick steps on the stairs, and

Dana swung the door open. His eyes scanned the old man slumped back on the chair, blood dripping from the black hole in his forehead. Saul found pity in Dana's face, partially for himself and partially for Gregory. Dana then walked to the table and grabbed the gun Benjamin had left on the table.

'What are you doing, Dana?' Benjamin said and extended his hand. 'Give me back the gun!'

'We need to throw the police off your trail.'

'Give me the gun, Dana. We're registered as dead people. They can't trace us.' He then took a step towards Dana.

'Stop!' Dana said and pointed the gun to his head.

'Give me the gun, Dana. Calm down.' Benjamin took another step.

'Marie loved you. Don't doubt that.'

'I know. Give me the gun. Please' Benjamin took another small step.

'Forgive me, Benjamin. But I had to help her.' Dana started crying. 'She would have done it, anyway. I know my sister. When someone decides you can never change their mind. Forgive me.'

'I'd already forgiven you.' Benjamin took another small step and almost reached Dana's arm. 'Let's talk. Give me the gun. Please'

'Forgive me, her, and yourself.'

Part 7

Saul helped Uncle Delbert remove weeds in the flower patch.

'The white ones are bruiseworts. The reds are corn roses,' Uncle Delbert taught Saul the name of the flowers.

'What are the blue ones called?'

'Scorpion grass.'

Saul and Uncle Delbert stepped back and looked with pride at their flower patch, which was now devoid of weeds after their grueling manual labor since breakfast. Once they stepped out of the flower patch, the lavenders started buzzing again with bees. Then they went back to recheck the hives, which two workers were busy surrounding with fences.

'Hope this can stop the honey badgers, ' Uncle Delbert said, leaning on his cane and wiping his brow.

'Gentlemen!' Dana, who reluctantly had to let go of his chic suit for more informal attire for the farm, shouted to them from a distance as he was afraid of the bees. 'Benjamin and Joel want to see you. They're in the main house.' However, even dressed in farmer's clothes, it was easy to tell Dana didn't fit in well. After the drama in the curator's office, when Benjamin took the gun from Dana's hands, the trio dealt with the issue in what they viewed as the healthiest way; pretending nothing had happened. So, Saul didn't ask him why he was asking for Benjamin's forgiveness. He did so not out of decorum but out of plain apathy. Recently, he felt nothing but anger or guilt.

As they entered the main house, Benjamin was sitting around the table reading the newspaper: 'HORROR: Beloved Temple Curator Killed; Suspects are at large. Read the other details and the note left by the killers on page 3'. Benjamin told Saul that he had left a note that was asking people to vote 'no' in the referendum, with the title 'Stop the Massacre.' Saul had his doubts about whether the note could change anyone's mind, but at this point, he cared more about hurting the people who took everything he loved. It was now about taking revenge. Finding someone he hated more than himself. Benjamin laid out the newspaper on the table and pointed to the headline:

'We need to capitalize on this. Today, we'll go back to the city and discreetly put pamphlets around about the referendum.' Saul nodded his head in agreement while Uncle Delbert did not deign to join the comment or even look at the newspaper but instead watched his flower patch from the window.

'I'm pregnant,' Kat announced as she entered the house holding Joel's hand. Benjamin jumped to his feet and gave them a hug. Saul sufficed with a big smile and a handshake with both. He was happy for Kat, especially since she had put an immense effort into giving Saul a prosthetic arm so he could go outside and pretend to be 'normal.'

'I read they're now using new machines to tell the gender of the baby.' Benjamin said as they took their seats around the table. 'Maybe you can ask for it next time you go for amniocentesis.'

'The doctor said it's too early to tell the gender,' Kat said. Saul could not help but notice she folded her arms around her belly. 'Was she always doing that, or is it instinctual?' he thought.

'Besides, we don't want amniocentesis,' Joel said and pulled his chair closer to Saul to see the newspaper.

'Why so, if I may ask?' Uncle Delbert chimed in without taking his eyes off the window.

'Yes, why not, Kat? You can learn whether the baby has any illness.' Saul asked and flipped to page three: '*Killers ask people to vote no in the referendum and stop criminalizing interference with other people's decisions regarding their life.*'

'I know what amniocentesis is, Saul,' Kat said in a harsh voice. Saul immediately noticed he'd struck a chord he'd not intended to. 'What do I do with the test results? Get an abortion if my baby has Down syndrome? Or what if she's missing a toe? How about an entire foot?' Kat then realized her word's implications. 'Sorry, Saul. I didn't mean to...'

'No worries. I didn't mean to... You know.' Saul said as he blushed and stammered. Uncle Delbert congratulated the couple again and walked outside.

'We know, we know. No worries.' Joel interrupted and snatched the newspaper from Saul's hand. 'We discussed it a lot too. Whatever happens, he will be our baby.'

'Or she,' Kat sneered and rubbed her belly.

'He'll be his father's boy.'

Saul and Benjamin rolled their eyes simultaneously and burst into laughter together, dispersing the built-up tension. Joel hid behind the newspaper and giggled. On the back page, Saul saw an ad: '*Hunting season is open again! Visit Proud Heritage Firearms to sign up for a hunting slot and earn a chance to win the new MU-X Rifle!*'

Saul then stepped outside to change his clothes before they headed for the city. He saw Uncle Delbert sitting on a stool, smoking a pipe.

'I regret not getting married, having kids. My parents loved kids. I wish I'd given them grandchildren,' Uncle Delbert said as he made smoke clouds with his pipe.

Saul didn't know how to react, so he stood in silence next to the old man. He nearly extended his hand to pat him on the shoulder but decided against it and instead put his palm on the wall.

'Was there someone you loved?' he finally muttered to break the silence.

'No. That's the annoying part, kid. I never fell in love.' Uncle Delbert stood up and put out his pipe. 'Don't worry. Just the gibberish of an old man. Let me see how the fence is coming along for the hives.'

As Uncle Delbert left and started climbing up the hill, Benjamin appeared behind Saul and squeezed his shoulder.

'Delbert is a good man, Saul.'

'I know. But regret is eating him up.'

'It's eating all of us up,' Benjamin said and spat on the ground.

***

As it became a habit of his that time, Benjamin had arrived late from the office. Way past the time happy families would have dinner. He opened the door, and Marie was already waiting for him in the entry.

'Finally!' Marie said. 'I was about to call the police to report you missing. Glad you found your way back.'

'I was working, Marie,' Benjamin huffed and hung his coat in the armoire. 'I told you so. I'm not playing games.' He tried to step inside the living room, but Marie rolled her chair and blocked him. Benjamin then noticed the mess in the kitchen: a pot of stew had fallen on the floor, which was covered.

'Oops,' Marie said and let Benjamin pass. 'I dropped the pot and couldn't clean it, you know,' she said and pointed to her legs.

Benjamin sighed and rolled up his sleeves. He was sure Marie did it on purpose as a punishment for him being late again. Even though he suppressed any verbal grievances directly at her, shaking his head and muttering to himself along the way to the kitchen was enough for Marie to pick up the cue.

'Ooh! I am sorry, Ben!' She yelled in a high soprano voice, without cracking, that would have made a trained singer jealous. She rolled her wheelchair into the kitchen past Benjamin. 'I'll clean it myself.' She then threw herself off the wheelchair, which flew back, hit a wooden stand, and knocked over a vase full of petunias. Marie hit the floor with a hard thud on her hands and started crawling to the kitchen.

'I'm sorry,' Benjamin rushed to his wife to lift her up. 'I was just tired. I was being a jerk. Please forgive me.' His voice cracked as panic and guilt overcame him. She pushed him back as she reached the mess on the floor.

'Let me go! I'll clean it, Ben.' While trying to get away from her husband, she threw a punch which punctured Benjamin's lip, and blood began gushing. Unfazed, Benjamin pulled her to his bosom.

'I'm sorry. Please,' he cried.

'You think I'm useless. Worthless. I wish the car had killed me.' Her words and tears struck Benjamin with full force.

'Shh. Don't say that.' Benjamin ran his fingers through her hair. He pulled back from her and kissed her on the forehead, smearing both of their faces in his blood. She wriggled in his arms to get away but did not put enough force into it this time, and he pulled her back to his bosom.

'I know why you're late. You hate me. You hate dealing with a half-woman who can't even open the door for you and throw herself in your arms. You see another woman. What's her name?'

'Don't be silly. I am sorry, baby. I love you. I promise I will never work late ever again.' Benjamin pushed her back to see Marie's eyes. 'You know, I don't see any other woman besides you.'

'Maybe you should.'

***

When Saul returned, Joel and Benjamin were loading the farm's pickup truck with bags of fertilizer. After they pushed the last bag into the trunk, Joel asked Benjamin to bring the car they were going to use to travel to the city.

At the city, they split up to go to different regions to distribute the pamphlets that said: 'Death is not Freedom: Vote no in the referendum.' Even though it wasn't illegal to campaign against the referendum, the 'no' camp was small enough to raise doubts about the connection between people distributing the pamphlets and the attackers in the city, so they reminded each other to be cautious.

As Saul wandered around the streets, dropping the pamphlets door to door, he realized his steps were leading him to Ezra's house. An image of Faye and Ezra kissing flashed before his eyes and burned his throat with jealousy. He wondered what she had made of him. Did she somehow know he was a murderer? He punched himself in the head to shake off the images and the concerns but couldn't get rid of the built-up guilt inside him for killing his mother. 'Yes. I killed her,' Saul murmured to himself and sat on the curbside. He now hated every sunny day filled with the joyous sounds of nature and people laughing as it seemed they were laughing at him. Now, he didn't regret what he did to Mrs. Pallas as he thought she had killed many others and would keep on doing so. But what was his action for if someone similar took her place instead?

A sparrow landed near him on the road and hoped toward the curb to peck something Saul couldn't see. He punched his knee in frustration, knowing how much his mother liked to watch birds. In everything good and beautiful, he saw her, as she was everything good and beautiful to him. His lungs shrunk once again, leaving him gasping for air. He wanted to take off the prosthetic arm and drive the long knife underneath to his chest to remove the darkness sucking him in. A flash of rage filled him. 'It's Ezra's fault,' he fumed to himself. 'If he'd told me about Sophie, we could have saved her.' He imagined Ezra laughing and waving to Sophie as she walked to the Farewell Tree. Led by the anger brewing in him, Saul once again rose to his feet to go to Ezra's house.

Once he arrived on the porch, his heart started pounding faster and faster. He just wanted a minute with Ezra to ask, 'Why did Sophie kill herself?' Maybe a punch afterward. But first, he wanted an answer. He rang the bell.

'Young man!' called a voice behind Saul, and turning, he saw a cop sticking his head out of a patrol car. 'Are you the one distributing the pamphlets?'

'Yes,' Saul said and hid his prosthetic arm behind his back, which made the cop squint to see what Saul was hiding.

'You shouldn't drop them at people's doors. That's littering. But you can hand the pamphlets in person.'

'Sorry. I will do so, sir.'

'Aren't your parents at home?'

'Oh no. This isn't my house.' Saul said, trying to get his voice under control. 'I was going to see my friend, but I guess he isn't at home.'

'Seems so,' the police officer said and pulled his head back inside the car. 'Have a good day.'

Once the police officer drove away, Saul threw the couple of pamphlets in his hand to a nearby trash can. He then pulled a newspaper clipping from his pocket:

"Proud Heritage Firearms: Olive Mountain Lane, No: 144."

***

On his way back to their meeting point, the bus stopped at a traffic light which was a block away from the city cemetery. Saul asked the driver to open the door, and he jumped out. As he wound through the streets leading to the cemetery, he noticed another woman who'd got off the bus at the same time started to follow him. He thought when the man in the brown suit that stalked him last time blew his cover, they sent another to track him. Saul didn't change his route and walked to the city cemetery, which was next to the Farewell Tree Park. In the shop windows, he glanced at the reflection of the young woman with the rose bouquet walking a couple of steps behind him. He felt his pulse rising in his temples and placed his hand on his prosthetic wrist, ready to unsheathe the long knife. Near the entrance, after confirming that no one was around to witness the confrontation, Saul turned back in a swift move to confront the stalker. The young woman, however, greeted him with a surprised smile and passed by.

Left in embarrassment and anger, Saul sat down on a bench and watched the woman kneel beside a grave and run her fingers over the marble. She then placed the flowers under the headstone and plucked the weeds growing around. If she had wailed and thrown herself on the marble, Saul would have found a momentary solace in her mourning. But watching her unwavering composure and dedication to clean around the grave, seeded an uneasiness in Saul's mind.

He looked at the path leading to his sister's grave. Next to it, he expected to see his mother's. 'Bury me here, Saul, when I die.' She would always point to the land beside his sister's. 'Next to my girl.' Now, he didn't want to visit their grave as it would shatter a secret hope that he didn't even want to reveal to himself that her mother might still be alive, and seeing her name on that grave would take the unspeakable refuge away from him. '*My dad's right. I'm a coward,*' he thought. '*I don't even have the courage to kill myself and end the suffering for everyone.*' His sister was the brave one.

He remembered a scene more than a decade ago when his and Ezra's family went on a picnic. A dog that had run away from its owner ran up to them, barking. Until their parents came to help them chase the dog away, his sister, who was at the most twelve back then, stood between the dog and them. 'Go away. GO!' She stamped her foot and shook her fist while Ezra and he cowered behind her. How much he would love to hide behind her skirt again.

***

The next morning, Saul followed Joel and Benjamin to the cowbarn.

'We have multiple cows pregnant. One is about to give birth.' Joel, with a rifle strapped to his shoulder, said and entered the barn first. A couple of workers inside the barn were leading the ten cows to the new milking machine. Once they left, another woman cleaned their enclosure.

Finally, the trio arrived at the enclosure of the pregnant cow, which was busy pushing hay around with its nose. After a couple of minutes of back and forth, the cow dropped to her side and tried to push the calf out. Seeing a birth for the first time, Saul could not help but feel sorry for the cow, who he thought must be in immense pain.

After failing to squeeze out the calf lying on the ground, the cow got up on her feet again, and after a bit of pushing, the front legs and the calf's nose appeared. Another push, then the calf dropped onto the stack of hay. Without enjoying the relief of birth, the cow went on to lick the calf's nostrils to help it breathe. A couple of minutes later, after seeing the calf twitch freely, the cow stepped aside and busied herself, eating the hay in her closure. Benjamin opened the door and, with small steps, approached the calf. The cow lifted her head to glance at Benjamin but, deciding he was no danger, lowered her head once again. Benjamin then reached the calf, still lying on the ground, and lifted its tail. He turned around to Joel and shook his head. Joel then opened the enclosure's gate, and Benjamin dragged the calf out. Invigorated by the tugging, the calf made its first attempt to stand on its feet, but Joel, in a single, fluent move, took aim at the calf's head and killed it. The sound reverberated in the barn for a moment but died down and startled the animals, including the new mother. Then they lowered their heads back to the hay in the feeders.

'What the hell, man?' Saul shouted after shaking off his initial shock, which took two seconds longer than the cows'.

'Well...' Benjamin winked at Joel. 'This is a dairy farm, and it's nearly impossible to milk a bull.' The pair giggled at Benjamin's joke.

'Why not raise it? Don't we need bulls, anyway?'

'We buy special bulls or just semen for reproduction.' Benjamin shrugged him off and asked him to walk to another enclosure.

'And cost-wise, it's cheaper to kill the male calves immediately,' Joel chimed in and reloaded his rifle.

'This cow here didn't get pregnant this year, so she's no use to us.' He then approached the enclosure and took aim at her head. When the cow was shot, Saul expected her to convulse or even somehow scream, but she just dropped to the ground without a sigh. Benjamin asked two workers to remove the carcass from the barn.

***

Nearly two dozen people, excluding the kids living on the farm, gathered in the main house, which felt stuffier and hotter than usual on this starless summer night. Glued to his chair, Saul kept an eye on the wooden walls and the ceiling to make sure they did not encroach on him any further than they already did. As the people's chatter got louder and louder, their voices assumed a solid form and filled all the remaining air, making it nearly impossible for Saul to breathe comfortably. Even the katydids were noisier, and the occasional fireflies outside the window were brighter than on a regular night, which overwhelmed Saul even further.

Benjamin entered the room and asked people to keep silent, a kind request followed by everyone except a newborn baby who didn't know any better. After an excruciating half hour, Saul finally took a deep breath. Benjamin stood up in front of the dead fireplace and crossed his arms on his chest.

'We didn't spell it out, but as you might have all guessed, we were the ones who killed the curator.'

'Good riddance!' the woman who started breastfeeding the boisterous baby shouted as a few others joined with cheers and laughter. 'Yes. He was the reason many good people took their own lives. Bravo!' another man said and started a round of applause.

'Referendum is still two weeks away. We are doing our best...' Benjamin started after calming the crowd but got cut off by another woman.

'You're doing jack shit!' Zoey, a pale woman in her thirties who helped to make cheese with the excess milk, had turned the darkest pink she could manage with rage. She was wearing a red-hued dress, which helped transmit her anger more to the receiver. 'Polls show still at least ninety percent will vote in favor.' She then took a break and fought against her cracking voice. 'I heard my sister killed herself yesterday.'

'I am sorry. Truly.' Benjamin said, leaning his back against the wall and lowering his head. 'I understand your pain. But we can't undo decades of brainwashing in three months. Can we?'

'Huh! So, you gathered us here to tell us we should give up and see our loved ones disappear?' Another man jumped to his feet and shook his fat finger in Benjamin's face. The baby, who had stopped sucking, started crying again. 'Shh. Shh' Her mother drew him closer to her chest. 'Shh. Shh.'

Saul fought the urge to run away.

'Let the man finish!' Joel snarled and hit his fist against the wall, sending a loud thud across the room. 'We are all on the same team, people!' Kat pulled him down by his arm and made him sit back. The man with the fat finger opened his mouth, but a woman sitting next to him also hauled him down. Benjamin then pulled out a paper and held it up so everyone could see.

'We have acquired the names and addresses of people who are going to commit suicide by the Farewell Tree next week. By committing suicide there publicly, they are being part of the city's propaganda to further the misery and irradicate the suffering in societal consciousness.' Benjamin said as everyone, including the baby who had started sucking his mother's breast again, fell silent. 'We're going to kill these ten people to stop the propaganda and take back the control. We will make people wake up from this decades-long nightmare.'

***

The cacophony nearly snowballed to fisticuffs if not for an occasional invisible hand that pulled down the agitated party to remain grounded in civility.

'So, we're going to become murderers! I joined the farm on the promise to save lives, not to shovel manure!' The man with the fat fingers shouted over the commotion.

'They'll kill themselves even if we do nothing. Don't you understand, you idiot?' Joel, trying to get away from Kat's iron grip, shouted back at the fat-fingered man. Saul, who had been brooding in a corner, jumped onto his chair.

'SILENCE!' His throat burned with the sudden gush of violence. 'This is our last chance to do something. Is it a perfect plan? I don't think so. Are we able to change anything? Probably not.' He continued with a lower voice. 'If anyone has a better plan that can change the outcome of the referendum in the next two weeks. I'm ready to listen. But as Joel said, whatever we decide, those people will die anyway.'

'To have any chance to succeed, we need to stop the propaganda machine.' Benjamin took over and asked Saul to sit back down. 'People who don't want to get involved can leave the farm now. I would only ask them to keep silent.' His gaze scanned the room, but no one made a gesture to exit.

'We will torture no one, right?' the breastfeeding woman asked.

'No,' Joel replied.

'We have little time.' Benjamin said and started pacing around the room with small, rapid steps. 'We act tomorrow night. We will visit these addresses in groups of two. If we are successful, TV and all the newspapers will discuss our resistance. We have to make people think and understand how the city is killing them and their loved ones.'

'We want revenge for the people taken from us!' Zoey, whose face now matched her red dress, yelled. 'We want revenge!' others joined the chant, including the fat-fingered man.

***

Just at the break of dawn, Saul woke up from yet another nightmare. He was a little boy walking alongside his mother in the Farewell Tree Park. When they reached the tree, Daisy let go of his hand and pointed to the tree. 'Come to me, Saul.' He looked back at his mother's turquoise eyes. 'But I am already with you, Mom,' Saul objected. But his mother repeated, 'Come to me, Saul.' Her face was yet again hidden behind a translucent veil, but her eyes tore through the barrier and pulled Saul inside a freezing whirlpool, 'Come to me, baby.'

Saul walked to the beehives and sat under the birch copse, looking down at the farm enchanted under a summer slumber. Even the hive seemed dormant. Saul knew Sophie didn't intend her actions to be a tool for propaganda, but as Benjamin said, it was indeed undeniable that she helped to promulgate the poison further. He laughed to himself and thought. 'How well did I know Sophie to decide what her intention was?' He was angry at himself for intervening during the school trip. He would still have his arm, his mother, and his Poppy. 'I wish she'd died earlier,' he murmured. Lava spurted from his heart and melted any compassion he harbored for the living or the dead. 'It's all Ezra's fault,' he concurred at last.

'Someone woke up early,' Uncle Delbert greeted him and pulled him out of the hole he'd dug. Saul sufficed with a faint smile and a nod to the man, who sat down and lit his pipe. The acrid smoke tingled Saul's nose as Uncle Delbert took a deep breath and rested the back of his head on the tree trunk.

'I quit my job on a sunny morning like this one. On that spring day, the breeze filled my room with a subtle lilac scent, and I no longer wanted to marry.' As the horizon mellowed out to the color of a dandelion from the blood orange it had been, the heart of the farm beat again to invigorate the souls and unleash them from their night-long drowsiness. 'We had abolished retirement. So, I felt really hopeless. Do you know what retirement is? I can't keep track anymore of what young people know or not,' Uncle Delbert chuckled to himself and drew another breath from his pipe.

'I heard people used to not work after a certain age,' Saul said.

Uncle Delbert then managed to blow a smoke ring for the first time. His face lit up with childish excitement, and he tugged Saul's sleeve to show the boy the fleeting shape. Uncle Delbert was going to remember it forever.

'Yes, they used to, but not anymore. Benjamin's father, who also worked in the municipality as the chief architect who designed the city, was my friend. Through him, I ended up on the farm.' Uncle Delbert tried again to create a smoke ring but failed this time.

'If you couldn't work anymore, you were expected to kill yourself, weren't you?'

'Yes. I was.'

Benjamin emerged below and asked the pair to come down. Uncle Delbert pointed to his pipe and asked Benjamin for a couple of minutes longer.

'Do you know the story of the Farewell Tree?

'Yes. Benjamin told me the real version and explained how we're taught propaganda in school.'

'Huh. It's all lies. My father used to be a historian in the municipality. Jus Primae Noctis is a total myth. A tale created by philosophers to extoll the virtues of democracy.'

'What about the Farewell Tree then?'

'There was a feud between the blacksmith and the local vassal; that's true. My father found the court documents in the archives. But the court documents tell that the blacksmith was a drunkard who tried to kidnap the farmer's daughter. As a punishment, the vassal had ordered the blacksmith to be hanged in the Farewell Tree. The farmer gave away his daughter as a gift to the vassal. Later on, both sides embellished the story as they saw fit.'

'If we're to believe in the court documents.'

'Yes.' Uncle Delbert said, drawing another deep breath from the pipe and exhaling another smoke ring. 'Now, thinking about it, you're right. Probably, those are lies, too. Some people believe we used to live in harmony in ancient times. You know, when we were just cavemen. Nowadays, others argue that we're getting more civilized and peaceful.'

'What do you think, Uncle?'

'We have always been, and will be, the same pieces of shit. Excuse my language.' Uncle Delbert then fell into a coughing fit.

***

The bus driver had told Saul it was a short walk from the corner where he dropped him. But in retrospect, the boy wished he had asked what the driver meant by a short walk. After dragging his feet for half an hour on the asphalt under the sun, he started doubting the man's ability to judge what constituted a short walk. Definitely not this. Once he finally reached the overpass the driver had mentioned, Saul took a right turn onto a red clay road with fresh tire tracks. After a ten-minute walk, he saw a couple of cars parked down the road. He then headed up a small hill on the left to get a better look at the area. As he climbed the hill, weeds brushed past his legs, and Saul prayed that the tingling sensation on his skin wasn't an early reaction to the histamine injection of a stinging nettle.

Near a bush, he kneeled down and pulled out the binoculars he had borrowed from Joel. A short walk from the cars, he saw the hunting party's main camp, where about a dozen people drank from cans and a few others lined up in front of a booth signing some papers. His prey was nowhere to be seen. Yet.

After swatting away a rather large grasshopper from his leg, Saul pulled the marked map showing hunting zones which he got from the rifle store. It had been a while since he read maps during his time in the Boy Scouts, so it took him a while to figure out which direction to go with the aid of his compass. Heading towards the southwest, he then crouched and slid from the other side of the hill and crossed a knee-deep small stream.

After tracking a creek that branched off from the stream, Saul arrived at a derelict stone bridge. The map showed a left turn from the bridge, and he was finally at hunting zone three. 'Where are you, Poppy?' Saul murmured to himself and scanned the area with the binoculars, but the thick bushes and leafy trees limited his vision.

A crack from a broken branch.

He jumped and hid behind the closest tree. Under his shirt, Saul pulled the gun he'd borrowed from Kat. With caution, he leaned to the side and took a peek at the direction of the noise, where he saw a lone buck. The buck raised its head and sniffed the air but, detecting no danger, lowered its head back to the grass. Saul sighed with relief and hid the gun under his shirt again.

A shot rang out in the forest.

When Saul turned back to the buck, he saw the animal lying on the ground. He crawled behind a bush and took out his binoculars. A rifle-carrying figure in a hunter's orange vest appeared from behind the trees. 'Poppy,' Saul said to himself and took out the gun under his shirt.

The girl kicked the animal, and upon seeing no movement, she dropped the rifle beside the carcass and pulled out a hunting knife. As she kneeled down to field dress the buck, Saul approached from the side, behind the oak trees.

'How convenient for an accident,' Saul said and pointed the gun at her. Poppy raised her head for a moment but lowered her head to keep on working on the carcass. Now, she was removing the evidence of sex. 'I mistook the horns for pronghorn, but it turns out it was the devil herself,' Saul said.

'There are no pronghorns in this part of the world.'

'No objection to the devil, then?'

'You know me, I've always been humble enough to accept compliments,' Poppy said and wiped the sweat off of her brow, but she also ended up smearing a bit of blood on herself in the process. She moved her right knee to feel for her rifle, which was now under the carcass. A ray of sun bounced off the barrel of her rifle and into her eyes.

'Tsk, Tsk. I don't think you're that quick,' Saul said and took a couple of steps closer to her. Inside the forest, the pair was stuck in an encircling vacuum. They heard nothing but the knife slicing through the skin of the carcass, Saul's footsteps breaking off branches, and the sound of each other's breath. 'Where did we leave off? Hmm. Ah! You were about to tell me why you lied to me. Why you killed Sophie. Maybe also how you concocted the plan with Ezra.'

'What of Ezra? What are you rambling about?' Poppy asked, reaching for the diaphragm and starting to pull the guts out.

'Don't play dumb!' Saul said and fired a shot close to the carcass. The shot echoed through the forest, and a deer took off. 'Answer me, Poppy!'

'I cared about you!' Poppy said and threw the hunting knife, which stuck in the trunk of a tree near Saul's face. Out of the corner of his eye, Saul caught his distorted, bloodied image on the blade. He was caught in a blood pool, drowning. 'You needed closure! We needed it!' Poppy thumped his chest and kicked the carcass. 'You can't blame others for what happened. For your decisions. Even for others' decisions.'

'We could have saved her, Poppy.'

'From what? How many times? What about others?'

'We can save them all if we can just stop this damn referendum.'

'You're delusional. I see that there's nothing left inside you of the boy I once loved.'

'It's your fault! Your fault that Sophie died. Your fault I lost my arm. Your fault that my mom died,' Saul screamed and started crying.

'Is that why you're here with the gun in your hand? To fix a fault?' Poppy said and spat on the ground. 'Like a coward.'

'I loved you,' Saul said and took a step back. In the distance, a commotion rose, and they heard people coming. While the boy was distracted, Poppy knelt, grabbed his gun, and pointed it at him. Saul looked back at Poppy. His eyes gazed from her wavy chestnut hair to her adorable freckles, now mostly hidden under blood.

'I didn't deserve this,' he mumbled and pointed the gun at his temple. 'I wish I hadn't been born. I wish I'd never met you. That you never killed Sophie.'

'Go away, Saul. I don't want to see you.'

***

It was as hot as any other mid-summer night, but shivering in the car, Saul pressed his teeth together so they didn't chatter. He hugged himself and hunched forward to rest his forehead on the dashboard. Zoey, who had switched from the red dress to a t-shirt and jeans more fitting for the occasion, drove the car, paying no attention to Saul's misery. They were a few minutes away from their target, a wealthy lawyer in his forties, Mr. Huxley, who had an appointment with the Farewell Tree four days later. Zoey pulled the car in front of a white villa and confirmed it was the address written on the card Benjamin gave them. Saul guessed there must be a sort of party or family gathering in the well-lit house, which was filled with a multitude of ephemeral silhouettes appearing behind the curtains.

'I'll leave the car around the corner. Then tell him our battery is dead and needs jump-starting,' Zoey said, pulling a pistol out of the glove compartment, sticking it in her belt, and covering it with her t-shirt.

'If he doesn't cooperate… What will we do?'

'Improvise,' Zoey said and stepped out of the car.

'Fan… tas… tic.'

'Any better ideas, freak? Don't keep it to yourself!'

'Don't you dare call me a freak!' Saul stepped outside the car and slammed the door.

***

Zoey, wearing her most innocent face, knocked on the door and took a step back. Saul squeezed his prosthetic hand in his pocket. A curvy young blond woman opened the door, holding a baby in one arm.

'Hello?' she said, and a narrow-faced man in his early forties appeared behind her. 'Who is it?'

'Sorry to bother you late at night. My brother and I were driving, but our car stopped, and now our battery is dead, and it won't start.' Zoey recited the story she'd made up in a quick, fluent fashion. 'Can you help us jump-start it, please?' she asked and pointed to the lawyer's car outside the villa.

'Of course!' the woman said and asked the man, who moaned loudly and cursed under his breath, to fetch the keys. 'Don't mind him,' the lawyer's wife said, who was now embarrassed by her husband's surly behavior. 'He is a bit tired today.'

'No worries. Thank you, ma'am, thank you,' Zoey said and bowed her head.

Mr. Huxley and the pair drove the short distance around the corner where Zoey had left their car. The lawyer parked the car in front of it and opened up the hood.

'You should get your car checked so it doesn't abandon you in the middle of the night next time,' Mr. Huxley lectured them with an air of authority. 'I don't have all night. Please hurry and open the hood.' Saul went to the driver's side of their car and pretended to look for the lever to open up the hood.

'Thank you, Mr. Huxley,' Zoey said. 'We're truly sorry to bother you.'

'How do you know my name? Were you my client before?' The lawyer asked and took a more careful look at the pseudo-siblings. 'Let me help your brother open up the hood,' he said and took a step forward, but Zoey moved in front of him and blocked his path. The lawyer took a step back with a confused expression.

'Are you going to drive by yourself to the Farewell Tree? You would need a co-driver to fetch the car back,' Zoey said and put her hand on the pistol under her shirt.

'What?!' the lawyer said and took another step back to approach the driver's side of his car.

'You heard me.'

Saul stopped pretending to look for the lever, as he honestly didn't know where it was.

'Who are you? Are you working for the municipality?' the lawyer yelled and, regaining his composure, took a step forward to tower over Zoey, who, in a quick move, pulled the pistol from her belt.

'Get in the car!'

'No,' Mr. Huxley said and took another step forward. Zoey, trying to keep her distance from the lawyer, walked backward but hit their car and aimed the pistol at the lawyer's head.

'We need to talk to you. Either you be a nice guy and get in the car with us for a quick chat, or I will kill everyone in the house, starting with your wife and the baby.' Zoey straightened her posture and cocked the gun. 'Try me.'

'You don't know who I am!' Mr. Huxley hissed. 'You idiots will be in jail for the rest of your lives.'

'Saul, come here,' Zoey called and handed the pistol to the boy. 'I'll drive the car. You accompany our guest in the back seat.' Saul took over the weapon and asked the lawyer to get in the car. After the lawyer took his place, Saul got in from the opposite door while trying to keep his aim on the lawyer, who had switched from threatening the pair to bribing them.

'Do you want money? I'll pay twice whatever they are paying you.'

'You were going to die four days later. Why did you start caring about your life now?' Zoey asked and drove the car onto a path leading inside the woods. She then asked the lawyer to step out. Slowly. Carefully.

The trio gathered in front of the headlights, which pierced through the night to create room for the killing. Saul lifted the pistol to aim for the lawyer's head once again.

'You have a nice family. You're successful and rich. What's wrong with you?' Saul asked the lawyer, who felt the iciness from Saul and started shivering himself.

'We're not here to ask questions, Saul,' Zoey hissed. 'This idiot was even going to leave his baby behind. Either do it...' She then took a step towards Saul and opened her palm, '... or give me the gun.'

'Please, show mercy,' the lawyer said and dropped to his knees. 'I have a family.'

'Ha. Ha. Do you think about your family *now*?' Zoey hissed. 'We need to get back, Saul.'

'Please. I didn't know any better. I couldn't cope with the stress. I'm sorry. Give me another chance, please.' the man buried his face in his hands and began to sob.

'I can't,' Saul said and lowered the gun. Seizing the opportunity, the lawyer sprung at Saul, who turned out to be quicker than him, and fired a single shot at the man's head.

Upon seeing the dead man's open skull, which revealed all of its contents, Saul started vomiting. Zoey spat on the guy and yanked the pistol out of Saul's hand.

'Let's get back to the farm.'

***

Benjamin asked Kat to keep the engine running and stepped out of the car. As he climbed up the porch stairs leading to the house, he wore a charming smile to disarm the occupants. With his knuckle, he knocked three times on the door and then took two steps back. After he heard someone coming to open the door, he once again tapped his jacket to feel the long blade and the gun underneath it.

'Hello?' a middle-aged bald man with a red bushy beard answered the door.

'Sorry to disturb you late at night, sir. My name is Herman. I'm the father of one of the girls in your daughter's classroom. My daughter missed school last week and said your daughter might give her notes to copy. Can you bring her down for me, please?'

'I think you're mistaken, Mr. Herman. I don't have a daughter. Not anymore, at least.'

'Is this not Faye's house?'

'It's the next house,' the man pointed to the house next door.

'My apologies,' Benjamin said and gave a slight bow. 'Sorry to disturb you.' The man closed the door without acknowledging the apology. Benjamin walked down the porch and saw Kat gesturing to him from the car and asking what happened. He sufficed with mouthing okay to let her know everything was under his control.

He then knocked on the door of the red-bearded man's neighbor. A moment later, a teenage girl holding a crocheted bee opened the door.

'Good evening, sir.'

'Hello, young lady. Are you Faye?' Benjamin asked and took a small step towards her.

'Yes.' Faye replied, and a woman shouted from inside the house, 'Who is it, Faye?'. As the girl turned her head inside to answer the question, Benjamin unsheathed the long knife under his jacket with his right hand and pulled the girl by her shoulder with his free hand. Before the girl could react, Benjamin drove the knife into her chest three times in quick succession.

A woman from inside the house shouted again, 'Who is it, Faye?' But because blood filled the girl's mouth and lungs, she couldn't answer the question. Benjamin pulled the knife out of her chest and ran to their car to head back to the farm.

Faye dropped to her knees but held on tight to her crocheted bee. As a wave of dizziness enveloped her, she relived the moment that broke her heart the most and hurt more than the steel.

'I crocheted this for you,' she said and gave the girl sitting next to her on the park bench an otter.

'You're so lame.' the girl laughed. Faye blushed and pulled back the toy to her chest. 'I'm just joking. I love it,' the girl said and took the toy from Faye.

'I love you,' Faye said and leaned towards to kiss the girl. Faye buried her hand in the dark silk hair and pulled her head closer. The girl put her hand on Faye's soft, slim neck and squeezed enough to feel her pulse. Just before their lips met, the girl pulled herself back.

'This is not okay.' She shook her head and pushed away Faye. 'This is sickness. We are sick.'

'I love you,' Faye said and reached to hold her hand.

'Don't!' the girl said and stood up. 'No. No. Someone might see. No. No. What would people say!'

'You don't love those boys,' Faye replied and stood up, as well. She then extended her hand once more to the girl.

'Well. I don't love you either.' The girl turned her back and started walking away.

'Sophie, don't go.'

***

Everyone, except for two, was already back on the farm when Saul and Zoe arrived. Assassins had gathered in the main house and were sharing their stories. Benjamin, who was beaming, also invited Saul in, but the latter declined the invitation and directly headed for bed. After tossing from side to side for an hour, Saul gave up on trying to fall asleep and let the gory murder scene haunt his consciousness instead of his potential nightmares. Suffocating in his room, he then headed for the stables.

Just outside the stables, Uncle Delbert, who had stayed on the farm for the night because of his old age, was cleaning his pipe of old tobacco residue.

'You can't sleep either, huh?'

'It's really humid.'

'I always liked night more. During the day, you can only see what's there. But after dusk, you start to see what is not there as well.' He then pointed towards the dark forest.

'What?'

'Don't mind me,' Uncle Delbert giggled. Saul sat beside the old man and got lost in the faraway galaxies above them. When he pulled himself out of the Little Bear, he noticed two stars appearing on the forest road leading to the farm. Shortly thereafter, a galaxy of sound followed them.

'POLICE! YOU ARE UNDER ARREST!' The sound boomed through the night. 'DON'T MOVE!' A dozen police cars filled the main farmyard one by one. People scrambled out of the main house with guns in their hands and opened fire on the police, who retaliated in return.

Saul threw himself on the ground and crawled to the back of the stables. From there, he saw Joel step into the headlights from the main building with his rifle. He took a shot, and a police officer let out a cry. As Joel aimed for another target, he was hit in the chest and dropped his rifle on the ground. Kat ran towards her husband, and Saul heard the highest pitched, most bestial, and otherworldly scream in his life and froze on the dry grass. He felt the ants, which were not interested in human affairs, crawling on his fingers and face. As Kat's screams became muffled and dropped to a lower pitch, Saul kept moving towards the back of the stables.

He crouched behind the wooden wall and looked back at the farm lit by police headlights, occasional gunfire exchanges, and human screams mixed with those of the animals could be heard. Chaos to end all chaos.

Two police officers approached the other end of the stable and pointed their guns at Uncle Delbert, who, up to that point, was watching the macabre scene unfold before him. 'HANDS UP!' Uncle Delbert pushed his knees to get on his feet but lost his balance, leaned forward, holding his chest, and slumped face down on the ground. The officers rushed towards the old man, flipped him over to perform CPR, but declared him dead after a couple of strokes. Another police officer, with a flashlight and gun in hand, appeared behind his colleagues and walked towards the other end of the stables.

Saul crawled on all fours around the stables and saw an open window. By stepping on a nearby haystack, he threw himself into the stable. He hit the ground with a thud, which startled the nearby horses. Ignoring the pain, with a sudden rush of adrenaline, he got on his feet and went to the other side of the stable to see the dying-down scene playing outside the main house. People were being arrested by the police, and the wailing, scared children tugged their mothers' skirts.

'Search the barns and stables!' The police chief shouted to the officers around him. Saul felt as if his heart was beating inside his brain and drowning any idea he tried to think of, apart from one that echoed inside his skull: '*I don't want to die here.*'

He ran inside the stable to see if any horse had a saddle on. He hurtled towards the tack room but realized he didn't have time to saddle one, especially single-handedly. In frustration, he punched his left shoulder, which helped little with the predicament he found himself in. He ran back to the stable and got on the only horse with a halter. As he struggled to maintain his balance on the horse, two police officers entered the stable through the tack room. Seeing he had no time left, Saul smashed through the swinging gates of the stable at full canter. Shaking off their initial shock, nearby police officers started firing shots after him.

Saul buried his face in the neck of the black mare as he sped through the police cars, bullets whistling by him. For an instant, on his left in the crowd, he saw the man in the brown suit, wearing a police uniform now, who had followed him in the city alongside the fat-fingered man, now in handcuffs. Another police officer shouted at his colleagues: 'Release the dogs!'

Without the saddle and with only a single hand on the halter, Saul knew he was eventually going to slip. As his fear of being shot by the cops or bitten by the dogs exceeded his fear of being trampled by the horse, he still made the mare go at full gallop. 'Come on, baby, come on.'

Saul had his eyes on the grove surrounding the northern side of the farm. As they got away from the farm, they were plunging into darkness. Saul slowed the horse down to a canter, and then he saw the fence surrounding the perimeter. He didn't know how to make the horse jump over the fence and whether the animal would do it on its own. Before they were about to crash into the fence, the horse came to a halt and reared, making Saul slide and fall to the ground.

Saul felt a sharp pain in his right ankle but got up at once when he heard the dogs coming after him. He squeezed through the fence and threw himself into the woods with the moon as his only light to find his way. He sprinted, tried to pick up speed, straight towards where he assumed the highway must be, whose street lights became visible after a minute.

With the police dogs behind him, though his lungs burned and his spleen felt about to explode, he pressed on through the darkness until he tripped over a tree branch and fell on his knees. Before he could caress his bleeding knee, he heard barking, and a silhouette appeared behind the trees. Saul tried to stay still, not to make any noise, but the dog sniffed his sweat and ran towards the boy. Saul removed his prosthetic arm, and when the animal plunged on him, he swung the long knife attached to his stump. As he fell back with the impact, he heard the dog cry out in pain. Saul dropped to his knees to search for his prosthetic arm and found it near the animal, which was whining and twitching. Saul stabbed the animal thrice in the abdomen out of frustration.

He kept running towards the lights of the empty highway when he heard another dog barking behind him. Saul pressed on with his full power, but the dog soon caught up with him on the edge of the highway. The boy turned around to cut down the dog like the last one, but the canine acted quicker and sank her teeth into his right ankle. Blinded by the pain, Saul swung the blade, cutting both the dog's back and his left thigh. As he lifted his hand again to stab the dog, the pair were blinded by headlights. After being stabbed, the animal's grip weakened, and Saul was able to pull his leg away. As he turned around to the car, he saw a man approaching him with a pistol. 'Please, don't kill me'

The man took aim at the injured dog and killed it with a single shot. When the man took another step, Saul realized it was Benjamin with the truck.

'Can you walk?' Benjamin asked and lifted the boy to his feet.

'Yes,' Saul groaned and leaned on Benjamin as they shuffled towards the truck. 'How did you find me?'

'I saw you getting away on the horse. The chaos you created gave me a window of opportunity to drive away with the truck.'

'Anyone else manage to get away?' Saul threw himself in the passenger seat and almost fainted when he looked at his bloodied leg.

'No.'

Part 8

When a man rightly sees his soul,
he sees no death, no sickness or distress.
When a man rightly sees,
he sees all, he wins all, completely

— Samaveda, *Chāndogya Upanisad*

It became a thrill to even go outside to see the sun. Saul knew it was only a matter of time before the police caught them. *'How long can we hide here in Benjamin's house before a suspicious neighbor or a passerby reports us to the police?'* he asked himself. Part of him wanted to get caught, to let the hammer of justice fall on them, as he believed he deserved punishment. If not for the killing of the lawyer or Mrs. Pallas for killing his mother. He sought the punishment as a way of reconciliation with himself to be free of a burden heavier than the one Zeus had condemned Atlas to carry. *'Why did Atlas not let go of the heavens to be crushed underneath it, to end his eternal suffering?'* he wondered. *'Did he hope for a rescuer?'* Another part of Saul didn't care about anything anymore. He could have sat on the couch forever.

Meanwhile, Benjamin spent hours in the garage working on the truck for God knows why. He didn't bother to ask his rescuer. He laughed at the term. What did Benjamin rescue him from? *'I should have rotted in prison or, better yet, hung myself there,'* he thought, but *'I don't have the courage,'* he confessed.

Benjamin appeared out of the garage and headed to the bathroom once again. Since they moved in, Benjamin had again spent hours washing his hands. Saul intended to suggest Benjamin use gloves but, later on, decided not to intervene. It wasn't his business.

Saul turned on the TV to drown the voices from the bathroom and his mind. 'Good Evening. Hypocrisy continues.' The news anchor read from the teleprompter in front of her with apathy in her voice. 'Another member of the terrorist group, known for their attacks on the people with appointments with the Farewell Tree, killed herself. The woman identified only as K. by the police was pregnant when she...' Saul switched to another channel to see whether there was any movie playing. Benjamin dried his hands and sat alongside him on the sofa. They caught the last scene of a movie in which a man stormed a castle to rescue his daughter from a humanoid monster. The man picked up an iron spear, threw it with full force, and pierced the monster's chest with it. However, the creature laughed at the spear stuck in his chest and approached the couple to kill them. Just in the nick of time, a lightning bolt struck the spear and incinerated the monster.

'Happy ending,' Saul said.

'Yes. He saved her. The end. They lived happily ever after,' Benjamin replied. 'Happily. Ever. After.'

***

Marie rolled her wheelchair to the door to see her husband off to work. Benjamin put on his shoes and then leaned over the doorstep to give a kiss on his wife's right cheek. Then he leaned over to her left cheek but bit her instead.

'Ouch!' Marie cried out and leaned forward to catch Benjamin by his collar, but the latter proved nimbler and evaded her grasp.

'Better luck next time, Marie.'

'You'll pay for this,' she said, still rubbing her cheek.

'It's not my fault you taste delicious.' Benjamin laughed and ran his tongue over his lips.

'You should also try my fist. It's really appetizing as well.'

'Maybe next time,' Benjamin said and stepped down the stairs.

'Ben?'

'Yes, dear.'

'I love you.'

Benjamin climbed the steps back and blew a kiss to his wife. 'I love you too.'

After seeing Benjamin drive away, Marie called her brother Dana to come pick her up to drop by the hospital.

'Why aren't you asking Ben to drop you off?'

'I told you, he's busy. Are you going to help or not?'

'This is the second trip. You're getting me worried. Are you sick?'

'It is a girl's issue, I told you. Ask one more time, and I'll go into details that you'll regret.'

'Marie, can't you call a taxi?'

'Am I being a burden to you?' Marie shouted. 'I would have gone myself if I could!'

'No. No. Don't say that. I'm sorry. I didn't mean to... I'm on my way. Sorry.' Dana tried to compile a haphazard apology.

After thirty minutes, Dana, dressed sharply as ever, picked up his sister, and they were on their way to the hospital. He noticed Marie fidgeting with her thumbs, a habit from her childhood, which Dana picked up as a sign of distress.

'Are you okay?' Dana asked and threw a side glance at his sister, who had noticed she was fidgeting and settled her fingers on her lap instead. 'Problems with Benjamin?'

Marie deflected the question with a deadly glare and rolled down her window. 'With a brother like you, no one can give me a problem.'

'Ha. Ha. Ha.'

'I don't smell cigarettes. Did you quit?'

'I did. I've decided to enjoy the finer things in life instead. Such as the joy of having such a lovely sister.'

'Ha. Ha. Ha.'

Once the siblings arrived at the hospital, Dana first carried Marie in his arms into the hospital and then brought in her wheelchair. Marie asked Dana to sit in the waiting area as she left for her appointment. Fifteen minutes later, a nurse came into the waiting area and asked Dana to follow her into another room. When Dana entered the room, he saw Marie lying on a bed and a nurse hunched over her, giving her an injection.

'What's going on here?' Dana asked Marie and looked around the room at the faces of the doctors and nurses. His sister pointed to the chair next to the bed and extended her hand for her brother to hold. 'Marie, speak!' Dana said and held her hand.

'I am sorry, brother. I lied,' Marie said and squeezed Dana's hand.

'What did you give her?' Dana jumped to her feet. 'Speak. Now!' He then began to walk towards the nearest doctor standing by the door.

'If you don't know how to behave, I will ask Security to remove you,' The doctor said and crossed her arms on her chest. 'We should leave you alone. You have...' she then checked her watch. '10 more minutes.'

'No!' Dana screamed. 'What did you do to her?' Dana tried to follow the doctors as they walked out of the room, but her sister pulled him back by his arm.

'Dana, please. I don't want to be alone,' Marie said and waved goodbye to the doctors. She then again pointed to Dana, who was still struggling to free himself from her grip to sit with her. 'I have terminal pancreatic cancer.'

'Marie, why did...' he started but was cut off by his sister.

'I can't fight anymore. I don't want to. I can't put you or Ben through any more problems. I asked for euthanasia'

'No. No.' Dana started crying and dropped to his knees. 'Let's call back the doctors. Let's talk first.' With each breath he exhaled to utter the syllables, he felt his own life fleeing away from him. As he again attempted to run to the door after the doctors, Marie pulled him back once more.

'Dana. Let it be. Please,' Marie said and began crying, too. 'I don't want to suffer anymore. I don't want you or Ben to suffer anymore because of me.' As she finished her sentence, a red-hot ball started choking and burning Dana's throat, who could barely breathe anymore. 'I have a last request for you, brother.' Dana lifted his head and looked at his sister, hidden behind the blur of his tears. 'Can you tell Benjamin?' Dana cried even harder. 'I love you, brother. Forgive me.' Dana tried to speak, but the iron ball stuck in his throat wouldn't let him say anything. He pressed his face to her sister's palm and kissed it repeatedly. Marie reached to his head with her other hand and ran her fingers through his hair. 'I love you, brother. Ask Ben to forgive me. Tell him that I love him.' Dana looked at his sister's face and saw her eyelids close, and the delicate fingers inside his palm go limp.

'I love you, Marie.' he muttered one last time and buried his face in her palm again.

After an hour of crying and a small dose of sedative injection by the doctors, Dana approached the reception desk to call Benjamin so he could come to the hospital to sign the documents and pick up the body of his wife. Even in death, there was no escape from bureaucracy.

'Hello, Benjamin. This is Dana'

'Hello. Dana, I need to go in to a meeting. Can I call you later?'

'I... broke my leg,' Dana said and put the phone an arm's length away from himself to breathe deeply a couple of times. 'I'm in the city hospital. Can you come pick me up?'

'Can't you call a taxi?'

'I am in great pain, Benjamin. Come. Please.' Dana said and started sobbing. He opened his mouth again, but flames had again enveloped his insides, so he only managed to let out a small shriek.

'Fine. Fine. I'll pick you up, and we'll go to dinner.'

As Dana put the phone down, someone gripped his shoulder.

'I'm sorry for your loss.' an old man said, to which Dana replied with an empty stare accompanied by a steady stream of tears rolling down his cheeks. 'Sorry for eavesdropping. But I wanted to say something.'

'It's okay,' Dana said, then started crying again. 'It's just...'

'It's hard to deal with it, no doubt. When the pain passes away, I hope it will leave its place gratitude that her suffering is over. Don't focus on your loss but on her relief.'

'I'm not selfish!' Dana said and wiped away his tears. 'I loved her.'

'I'm sure you did. And I'm sure she loved you as well.'

'My head hurts,' Dana muttered and threw himself on the couch in the waiting room. He then buried his face in his palm.

'Here's my card. Maybe you will stop by to chat when you feel better, the old man said and passed Dana a business card. Dana took the fancy blue card from the guy and gave it a quick glance before stuffing it in his pocket.

'Thank you, Gregory.'

***

Saul zapped to another channel. Back to the news. 'Annual Farewell Tree Parade preparations are complete. You can watch the events live tomorrow morning on Channel 6.' the anchor said and turned to her co-host. 'A nice chance of early celebration before heading to the polls the day after. Now the weather.' Saul turned off the TV.

'I'll leave early tomorrow. I have business to attend to,' Benjamin said, breaking the silence. 'If I'm ... caught. The house is yours.' Saul buried his head in his hands and sighed.

'Can't we leave, Benjamin?' he asked with begging eyes. 'Let's try to escape to the other end of the world.'

'I told you this plague has spread everywhere in the world. Or will have soon,' Benjamin said and tapped on Saul's chest. 'It's in us. You can leave, but I'll do everything I can to stop this.'

'We lost, Benjamin,' Saul said. Benjamin got up and headed to his bedroom. 'I am tired of running away.' Saul slumped back on the sofa. Benjamin turned around to look at the boy.

'I will *not* run away. Not anymore. Goodnight, Saul.'

'Goodnight.'

***

When he woke up the next day, Benjamin had already left. Saul found the old religious book Benjamin had been reading, left open on the dinner table. He had underlined a section: '*O Lord God, remember me, I pray thee, and strengthen me, I pray thee, only this once, O God, that I may be at once avenged of the Philistines for my two eyes.*'

Saul prepared himself toast and turned on the TV to watch the parade. A line of cars was going through the boulevard. On both sides, people lined up holding banners, waving flags, and cheering the cars passing by. Nothing had changed since the parade when his sister had killed herself.

This year, the city had even ordered a replica of the Farewell Tree, complete with its steel noose, which was now passing on a trailer. Once it passed by the protocol stand, the city officials stood up and applauded the replica, which the news anchor declared represented the soul of the city and the essence of the freedoms. Saul went back to the kitchen to get a glass of milk. When he returned, he noticed the procession of cars had come to a halt as a pick-up truck had stopped in front of the protocol. Saul squinted his eyes and got closer to the TV.

'That's Benjamin's car.'

Benjamin got on top of the car and shook his fist at the protocol, which broke into a small stampede. Nearby police officers pulled their guns and ran to the pickup truck. Finishing his tirade, Benjamin, who had probably been shot, dropped something from his hand, and the truck exploded in flames which enveloped the boulevard. The TV screen first went silent, then dark.

Saul sat back at the dinner table, picked up his leftover toast, and changed the channel. He caught the end of a movie which was set in ancient times. Guards rushed into a treasure room, only to find the dead body of a beautiful woman, covered in precious gems, lying on an elevated marble podium. Out of her bosom, an asp slithered and then fell on the floor. Another happy ending.

***

Saul had defeated his once big-time nemesis, shirts, as he could now button them as quickly as before he lost his hand. However, tying his shoes was still taking a bit longer than he would have desired. But he'd learned to live with it. His stump also did not hurt out of the blue anymore. He looked at himself in the mirror as he put on his jacket. The longer he studied the boy trapped in the mirror, the more estranged Saul became to him. 'Hello. Have we met before?'

He went downstairs to the now empty garage and picked up one of the full petrol containers he had bought for Benjamin. Before he headed outside to the bus stop, Saul glanced one more time in the mirror.

Saul got off the bus one block before the cemetery and stopped by the florist. 'Can you arrange me a bouquet of scorpion grass, please?' He buried his nose in the pink and blue petals, but the flowers didn't reward him with any distinguishable scent. A momentary rage and disappointment towered in him as his lungs exploded with betrayal. Why deny him the simple joy of a sweet scent? His rage collapsed at once as he exhaled.

A gentle breeze washed over his face, mixed with the warmth emanating from the pavement and the façades of the buildings. He listened to a nightingale sitting atop a rowan tree. He put the container on the ground and pressed the bouquet to his body with his prosthetic arm. Then he put his right hand on the trunk of the tree and listened to the bird. If it was not for the engine noises, honks, and pedestrians chatting with each other, he might have been able to decipher the nightingale's language. He felt one more minute would have been enough to understand the bird. But the harder he tried, the faster the chirping of the nightingale trickled between his fingers.

***

Next to Chloe's tombstone stood Daisy's. Saul untied the bow holding the bouquet and separated the flowers into pink and blue ones. The latter on his mother's grave, the former on his sister's. 'Happy Birthday, Chloe.' He ran his fingers over the engraving on the marble. 'C... H... L... O... E'.

'I didn't deserve this!' he screamed in the empty cemetery and punched the grass, killing a hapless ladybug. Another punch. Another casualty.

'Hello, Saul.'

Saul turned around to see Ezra standing with a bouquet of white roses in his hand.

'I missed the bus, so I arrived a bit late,' Ezra said, looking at his watch. '12:05. So, five minutes late.' He gave Saul a faint smile and took a cautious, small step towards his friend. 'It's good to see you.'

'How dare you come here?' Saul yelled and jumped to his feet. A foreshock passing through him heralded a continent-breaking earthquake, and suddenly, he was out of breath. 'It's all your fault,' Saul said, surprising himself as much as Ezra. 'It's all your fault,' he repeated once again with more conviction to persuade himself.

'What?' Ezra, who was confused, said and lowered the bouquet in his hand. 'I loved Chloe.' He then looked at Daisy's tombstone. 'I'm sorry for Mrs. Daisy. I am,' he said, lowering his voice and taking another step towards Saul.

'I know what you did. Don't play stupid!' Saul replied and pushed Ezra's shoulder. 'You killed Sophie. I know you were dating her. It was your fault.' Saul took another step towards Ezra, who dropped the bouquet. Saul tried to push his friend again, but this time, Ezra hit Saul's hand away.

'Did you lose your mind? What's wrong with you?' Ezra pushed Saul, who tripped on a tree branch and fell back. 'I loved her!' Ezra, ignoring the tears forming in his eyes, then thumped his chest.

'Why did she kill herself, then?'

'I don't know, Saul!' Ezra screamed back, tears pouring from his eyes. 'She broke up with me. Asked me to forget her.'

'Liar!' Saul jumped to his feet and threw a punch at Ezra's face. 'You killed her!'

Disadvantaged by being single-handed, Saul received far more blows than he dealt. Cursing each other, the pair were locked in a primitive dance of kicks and punches, which left both of them bloodied and the bouquet of roses stomped on.

Ezra connected another skillful punch to Saul's right ear and caused the latter to lose his balance. Saul caught Ezra by the collar and pulled him down, and Ezra fell on Saul, who kept throwing punches at the other boy's face. After two more punches, Saul's adrenaline drained away, and he noticed warmth emanating from the limp body lying on top of him. When he tried to push Ezra off him, Saul saw that his long knife had pierced through his prosthetic arm and impaled Ezra.

Seeing a bloody boy towering over a dead body, a woman visiting the graveyard screamed. Shocked, Saul turned toward the woman who fled the cemetery at once. He unstrapped the long knife from his shoulder and dropped it by Ezra's dead body, then picked up the petrol container he'd left by the tombstones.

***

The park was brimming with life as Saul ran through it. Families and friends were huddled around the banks next to the lake, enjoying the sunny mid-summer day. Young parents were struggling to push their strollers on the uneven surface while searching for a pleasant shade to rest. The younglings played as elder siblings kept an eye on unleashed dogs, frantically looking for their toys or simply chasing an unfortunate butterfly while running away from their owners. Across the commotion, where trees gave way for a small opening, a group of little kids were flying their kites.

The people who noticed the single-armed boy covered in blood running towards them got out of his way. 'What the hell is going on?' they whispered to each other. The young boy ran through the crowds, ignoring his burning lungs until he reached the Farewell Tree. He opened the container's lid and doused its giant trunk with petrol. 'Stop!' he heard someone shouting and saw three policemen running towards him. 'Stop!' He jumped on the stairs leading to the steel noose. 'Stop!' Saul took a lighter from his pocket. He lit the fire and threw it on the dry trunk, which caught in an enveloping fire whose smoke burned Saul's tongue and left a bitter taste in his mouth. The police officers running towards him pulled out their guns. 'Get off there! You're under arrest!' Born out of absurdity, a tired smile landed on Saul's face.

The steel noose, which had baked for hours under the sun, burned his fingertips. But Saul knew the pain would be over soon. 'Next time,' he whispered to himself and took a leap of faith.

The End

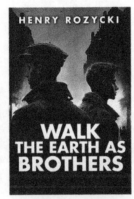
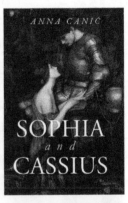
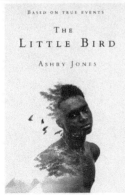

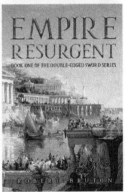